Rich Boy Mafia

D1316387

Rich Boy Mafia 4

A Novel By
DeMettrea

Rich Boy Mafia 4

Sullivan Productions Presents

Copyright © 2014 Demettrea

Editor Mike Covington

Acknowledgments and Dedications

First and foremost I want to thank my lord and savior, Jesus Christ. Without him nothing is possible. Thanks to my husband, Darryl Sr. who has been rocking with me through it all. You pushed and promoted and I appreciate you for it all. This is only the beginning; the sky is the limit.

To my kids, Alyse, Damar, Brandon, Darryl Jr. and Daniel, everything I do is for you.

Thanks to my granny who's there for me no matter what. I am still a spoiled brat because of you. Thanks to my mommy for promoting my work and being there through it all.

My girls, my rounds, my sistahs, where do I start? You all have been there for me. We have laughed together, cried together, and talked shit together. I couldn't have asked for a better set of friends. We share an unbreakable bond and I know this because many have tried to break it. Forever my sisters, Gio, Cassie Lola (Bandz), and Shay. I love y'all crazy asses till the death of me.

To my VIP section (Insider) You ladies are funny and you tell me the real. Erin Jasmine, Tenita , Victoria , Shaniqua , Kike

Shantay you messaged me and asked me to be your mentor and we became cool ever since that day .You have become my little sister in so many ways. You're so down to earth and sweet. Keep doing what you doing mama because you are destined for greatness.

Yanni, you have been with me since the beginning and I have had the pleasure of watching you grow into an amazing writer, I am so proud of you and can't wait to see you succeed even more. I love you little sis.

To Atiba, you know I rock with you all day. When I make it to the top you already know I'm bringing you with me. Your spot is already secured.

Lucy Dee I am so proud of you and honored that you chose me to work with. I see greatness in you. You are an amazing writer. Keep doing what you're doing.

To my Publishing family: Leo Sullivan, it is such an honor to work with someone so humble. I have been a reader of yours since Triple Crown and now to be a part of your team is great. To all my label mates: We out her y'all!

Thanks Shiana for answering my calls and doing what you do.

To my unofficial child, Cynthia: I love you.

To my sisters Taylor and Raquel, I love you babies. My brothers Juan and Dre I love y'all big heads.

Thanks to anyone that has read my work and told someone else about my work. You rock!

If I forgot you it wasn't on purpose. Charge it to my head and not my heart.

CHAPTER ONE

"So you still aint trying to give a nigga a chance," Stone asked Anise as they cuddled in bed. Anise didn't know what it's going to take for him to realize that they would never be a couple. It was just sex to Anise and nothing more. She could never give her heart to him because it belonged to another.

Monte and Anise had broken up a little over a year ago. However they remained friends. Anise just couldn't get over the fact that he had a baby on her. She understood that people made mistakes but her heart didn't understand that. Now, his daughter, Aniyah was a cutie and she spent time with her when Monte came around being that they had the same friends. It was impossible for them not to see each other. So the adult thing to do was suck that shit up and show his ass what he was missing.

"Stone I told you already that I am not looking for a relationship. I thought we both agreed that this was all it was. Please don't go catching feelings on a bitch." Anise got up out the bed and headed to the bathroom because she couldn't deal with Stone. Since splitting up with Monte she hadn't dated seriously and wasn't looking to. She was hurt to the core and wasn't ready to give another man the chance to hurt her again. She didn't even get in the shower. It was time to head home because Stone was in his feelings. There was no way they could be in a relationship. Plus, she didn't know how Lovely would feel about her boning her brother. Yes, Stone was her little secret.

Even though she knew Monte still wanted her, she refused to go there with him again. Now, Stone fine ass was her booty call. Even though he wanted more, that would never happened. He knew how to lay the pipe but Anise wasn't feeling a relationship with him. Whenever he got to talking that relationship shit she had to distance herself from him. Like today for instance. Shit was going good. They had just had some of the most explosive sex and he had to start that shit.

When Anise came out of the bathroom he was watching TV. She knew he was mad but it was what it was. She didn't have time to nurse his feelings.

"I'm out." He didn't respond but oh well. She grabbed her purse and headed out.

When she walked through the door she headed straight for the shower. She was drained mentally and physically. Even though she liked Stone she just wasn't feeling him the same way he was her. Monte had really fucked up for the next guy.

It had been a year and Monte was still calling and texting her. They were cool but he wanted to get back together and she wasn't hearing it. It only took one time for him to mess up and she wasn't giving him a second chance.

She lathered her body with Sweet Pea body wash and let the water run all over her. Her thoughts traveled to happier times in her life. While her feelings for Monte were deep and still there she also cared about Stone; just not enough to go all the way with him. She had become content over the past year with the way things were. She was at peace with it and just wanted to have fun. Monte had shattered her heart to pieces and she didn't think it would ever be pieced back together. Only time would tell.

After she got out the shower and dried off she put on some sweats and a tee. Today she was relaxing and leaving the bullshit behind. Anise prayed for better days to come.

Anise woke up to a text message from Monte. This was beginning to be an everyday thing. She debated on whether or not to open it. After a few minutes, curiosity got the best of her and she opened it.

Monte: what's up ma?

Me: what do you want Monte?

Monte: you

Me: not gone happen

Monte: I love you ma

"This nigga is tripping if he think it's ever gone be anything between us." she thought. She didn't even respond. It was time for her to get up and get her day

started. Just when she was doing fine he had to come along and stir up those feelings. She definitely needed to get out the house and get her mind on something else. She called Lovely to see what she was up to. Kimani's party was tomorrow so she was probably running around. While she waited for her to answer she looked through her closet for something to wear.

"Hey sissy pooh!" She answered all chipper.

"Hey boo. What the hell got you all happy?" Anise grabbed her white True religion baby tee and a pair of blue true religion jeans.

"Nothing, I'm just in a good mood. What you doing?" Anise heard London in the background calling for her daddy. That little girl was adorable.

"Well I'm about to come over because I'm bored out my mind and Monte keep texting me."

"Girl you need to just get back with him. Hell everybody makes mistakes. He loves yo ass, " Lovely replied. Anise knew it was the truth but she was good.

"Whatever Lovely, I'm not trying to hear that. Kiss my god baby and I'll see you in a minute." She hung up before she could reply. Lovely was always trying to get her back with Monte. But that was Lovely, always trying to make sure she was ok. That's why they were so close.

This past year had been one big rollercoaster after another. Monte really needed his baby girl back. You would think after a year he would be over her but he wasn't and didn't think he'd ever be. Anise was a down as bitch and he had fucked it up. Pussy will get a nigga fucked in the game every time. Monte never thought she would leave him. But jokes on him.

He sat in his office at Epiphany, the club he owned with Rahsaan and Phalon. This was where he spent a lot of his time just to get away from Kyah. She was the baby mama from hell. She constantly compared their relationship with his relationship with Anise there was no comparison. Anise was that deal and no one could replace her ever.

"Aye man you coming by the house later? We gone throw some shit on the grill and just chill," Phalon said as he poked his head in Monte's office.

"Yeah, I'm headed that way when I leave here," Monte told him.

"Aight man I'll catch you later." Phalon closed the door and Monte was once again left with thoughts of Anise. She had stopped responding to his text earlier so he decided to try his hand and call her. He needed to hear her voice even if for a minute. Her phone rang three times before she picked up.

"Hello?" Her voice was so soft and peaceful. Just what Monte needed to hear to put him in a good space.

"I just wanted to hear ya voice baby girl."

"Hey Monte. How are you?" He was surprised she was still on the phone with him. Usually she would have hung up by now.

"I'm good, just a little stressed. That's why I needed to hear your voice."

"Oh, I'm sorry to hear that. I hope everything gets better for you."

Just like her to say something sweet when a nigga was down and out. That's why he loved her. "Thanks baby girl, I love you."

"Bye Monte." Anise hung up. That hurt but he couldn't blame anyone but myself. He grabbed his keys and headed out. He had to get his mind right cause this shit was making him act like a bitch.

Monte jumped in his black Lamborghini Marcielago, something he'd bought just because and sped off towards Phalon's house. He turned the sound system up and Ace Hood blared through the speakers. He was on one and couldn't nobody tell him shit. It took him about fifteen minutes to get there. When he pulled up he saw Anise's car parked in the driveway and got excited. Monte shut the car off and got out. He walked a little faster knowing that his baby girl was on the other side of the door.

When he walked in Phalon was in the kitchen seasoning meat and he heard chatter coming from upstairs.

"What up man?" Monte greeted.

"Aint shit, ya girl upstairs." Phalon motioned towards the stairway.

"Good look." Monte headed upstairs to London's room where he heard the talking coming from. Lovely spotted him first and winked her eye.

"Hey Anise can you put her shoes on for me while I go check on Kimani."

"Yeah. Come on London, let auntie put on your shoes." Monte watched her with London and thought she was sexy as hell. *"How I fucked that up I will never understand"*. Once Anise put London's shoes on she tried to walk away quickly. He knew she probably smelled the scent of his Curve cologne and knew he was in the room without even turning around. He caught her arm before she could make her escape. London ran past both of them and they were now alone.

"Damn ma, you can't even be in the same room with me now?" Monte felt like shit. He hurt her that bad to where she didn't even want to be in the same room with him no more.

"What do you want Monte?" Her voice cracked. He pulled her in his arms and she tried to resist but he wasn't giving up that easy.

"Stop running from me ma." Monte held her tight and she finally stopped fighting. He thought about how good she felt in his arms. Monte knew he had to get that back and would die trying.

"Look at me baby girl." She took a minute but she finally looked up at him. The hurt he saw in her eyes fucked him up. He had fucked up a good thing over a night of passion.

"I can't apologize enough for hurting you but I hate to see you like this. I know we will probably never be together again but I want us to at least be friends. You are my heart and whether you believe me or not I love you and will always be here for you. Shit you still got a nigga paying bills and shit, that should tell you right there that you still number one." He joked and that got a smile out of her.

"You're right Monte. I forgive you. Now let me go punk." She playfully punched him in the arm. He grabbed her again.

"Keep ya hands to ya self, "he joked" She was now looking him in the eyes and he saw it in her face, she still had love for him. He bent down and kissed her lips, slowly and she moaned. After a good minute he fell back. Monte couldn't take it there with her only for her to go back to hating him. They were in a good space.........for now anyway.

"Come on let's go downstairs and help with the food." He grabbed her hand and they headed downstairs.

A few hours and a couple of drinks later, Monte was feeling nice. He sat and watched Anise kick it with her girls. The whole family had come over and chilled. One thing he saw that didn't sit well with him was that nigga Stone staring at Anise. He just let it go for now because he didn't need the drama and plus she wasn't his girl anymore. Fuck it. He decided to head out. He walked over to Anise to tell her he was leaving. He grabbed her around her waist and whispered in her ear.

"I'm out ma. I love you." He kissed her cheek before saying bye to everyone else.

CHAPTER TWO

Lovely was running around like crazy trying to get everything set for Kimani's party. Phalon had let her plan Kimani's party and she was loving it. Kimani wasn't her biological daughter but she was hers in every sense. Lovely was the one that was there when she had her first period last month. When she had nightmares about Kelly, Lovely was the one she came to. Lovely loved that little girl as if she gave birth to her.

Lovely was at Party City getting the last of the decorations. Kimani's favorite colors were pink and sky blue. So she had almost everything you can imagine needing for a little girls party. It helped that her hubby didn't give her a limit. Lovely usually didn't go crazy spending money but she was going all out for Kimani. After a few hours of shopping, she headed home. She wanted to get everything set up before Kimani came home. Ryan had took her shopping for her birthday so that Lovely could get everything ready. Phalon had London and Lovely had less than two hours to get everything ready and shower.

She decided to call Anise over to help me so that she could get everything done.

"Hey sissy pooh, what you doing?" She asked when Anise answered the phone.

"Girl just got dressed and headed to your house."

"Good because I need your help." Lovely laughed.

"I know that's why I'm on my way." Anise knew Lovely too well.

"Ok girl, I'll see you when you get here." She hung up and headed to the backyard to get started.

"Finally we're done and I only have about fifteen minutes to shower." Lovely said looking at her watch

"Go ahead I'll watch out for the guest," Anise said.

"Thanks girl." She headed upstairs to get showered and dressed for the party. London was sleep but she was already dressed. Phalon had put her down for a nap a little while ago.

It took Lovely about twenty minutes to get showered and dressed. She pulled her hair up in a ponytail and headed out back to get the party started. They had the pool ready, cotton candy, popcorn. They even had a spa area where the girls could get dolled up. You name it they had it. Phalon had started barbecuing the food as people started arriving.

"You did good ma." Phalon whispered in Lovely's ear as he walked up behind her. She was grabbing more refreshments for the kids.

"Thanks baby. I just wanted her to have the best birthday ever. Is she here yet?" Lovely asked.

"Ryan just called and said they were pulling up," Phalon informed her.

"Ok cool. Here help me carry this outside." Lovely passed him the case of juices and they headed outside. As Phalon was setting the drinks down Ryan and Kimani were walking in the backyard. She looked so cute in her outfit. She was rocking a sky blue and pink tutu, with a pink shirt that said *keep calm it's my birthday.* Her leggings were blue and she had on a pair of pink high top converse. She was real fly today thanks to step mama.

"Lovely, look what Auntie Ryan bought me." Kamani had about three bags from Justice in her hands. One thing she liked was clothes and she had plenty of them.

"How about you put your bags in your room and we'll look through it all later after the party ok?"

"Ok." Kamani ran in the house and it made Lovely feel good to see her so happy. Lovely didn't know how she felt about her mother being gone so she tried to fill that void as best she could without overstepping her boundaries.

"Hey girl." Ryan walked over to Lovely.

"Thanks for taking her shopping Ry, Lovely commended her."

"Girl it was nothing. You know I love to shop. King should be here with the kids soon. I think he was picking up Harley and Harlem Jr. too."

"Cool. Well the kids have started partying already so let's have fun." Lovely knew this was going to be a party to remember.

The party was in full swing and the kids were enjoying themselves. Anise didn't see how Lovely did it. All these damn kids and then she had to do it all over again in a few months for London's birthday. She sat near the pool away from all the madness. Every once in a while she would see Monte look at her as he held a conversation with Phalon. She tried to look the other way because it was just something about him that made her nervous. She didn't know why she couldn't get him out her head. It had been over a year and he was still in her system. She had to shake him and fast.

She got up and headed in the house. Anise couldn't take looking at him anymore. He was too damn fine. From his dreads that he had let grow out longer to his perfectly structured cheekbones. And that one damn dimple that poked out when he smiled. Damn she had it bad. She grabbed a beer out of the fridge because she needed something to calm my nerves.

"You ok sis?" Anise didn't even hear Lovely come in.

"Yeah I'm good ma. I'll be back out in a second." She was hoping Lovely would go back outside. Wishful thinking on her part. Lovely knew Anise better than she knew herself.

"Nah ma, what's the deal, " Lovely asked as she sat on the bar stool that was placed at the center island. Anise loved Lovely's kitchen. She looked around and admired the black and gray décor. It was bad ass.

"I'm just in my feelings, but I'll be cool." Anise replied keeping it short.

"Why don t you stop being stubborn and go get ya man," Lovely said with a raised eyebrow.

"It aint that simple sis." Anise shook her head. If only Lovely knew what she was really dealing with.

"Why the hell isn't it? You love him! Yeah,he fucked up, but people make mistakes. Don't let one fuck up keep you from happiness sis." Anise knew Lovely was right but it just wasn't that easy. She had always been stubborn and hated to be fucked over.

"Look I need to tell you something, and I don't want you to be mad at me sis." Anise didn't know how she would feel about her and Stone sleeping together but she needed to tell her. It was only right because that was her brother.

"I would never be mad at you sis, " she said and Anise knew she was being truthful. They had that sisterly bond and knew each other well.

"Stone and I have been kicking it, but it's nothing serious." She laughed but didn't find shit funny.

"Girl bye, I knew that. You are too obvious! But you need to dead that and I'm only saying this because your heart isn't with Stone, it's with Monte. I love you like a sister and that's my brother. I would hate for either of you to get hurt. Walk away from Stone and go where your heart is sis, " she said before walking back outside. Lovely left Anise thinking and as always she was right, but she still wasn't ready for Monte. She needed to get shit together with Anise first.

"You good ma?" That voice did something to her every time. The smell of his Armani cologne assaulted her nostrils and suddenly she felt like she was going to suffocate. Anise was so deep in thought that she never even heard him come in. Have you ever loved someone so much that it hurt? Well that's how she feel about Monte. The only issue was if she could get past what he did. That was a tough pill to swallow.

"Yeah, I came in to grab a beer." She held up the half empty beer bottle. He walked towards her and her breathing seemed to have stopped. She needed to get out of the kitchen with him but her feet wouldn't move. Her palms started to sweat and she got butterflies in the pit of her stomach. He was moving closer. He was now in her personal space. They were standing so close that their lips were touching. He kissed her. It wasn't sexual or even intimate. It was sort of a *I'm here for you when you need me type kiss.* He walked away leaving her alone. This was going to be harder than she thought.

Monte couldn't help his self, her lips were looking like they needed to be kissed. He knew she was boning that nigga Stone but that didn't mean shit to him. Her heart was with him and that's something she couldn't deny. As long as it took though, he was willing to wait for baby girl. She thought he was with Kyah but that wasn't the case. They lived in separate houses, no sex, just co-parenting. Nothing more, even though Kyah wanted more.

Monte was sitting at the table with Phalon, Javon and Trina. They were about to get a game of spades going. Monte saw Anise come out the house and called her over to be his lucky charm.

"Come over here and help me win ma, " Monte requested.

Anise smiled as she walked over and pulled up a chair up.

"Calling her over here aint gone stop this ass whooping," Phalon joked.

"Nigga please! Put ya money up then, " Monte said pulling out a knot and slamming it on the table.

"Shit you aint saying shit my dude." Phalon pulled out a knot as well and they got the game going.

"Aye ma you see this hand." Monte leaned over in her space.

"Yeah you got this one." Anise replied.

"Don't gas that nigga head up sis." They talked shit and played a few games. Javon and Monte ended up winning two games and Phalon and Trina won three. It was all fun though. Even better for Monte because Anise was next to him and she was talking to him and that was all that mattered.

CHAPTER THREE

Monte was fucked up messing around with Phalon and them. He didn't even remember how many drinks he had. All he remembered was strippers and singles. He had tricked off so much money at Ace of Spades it wasn't funny. It was after three in the morning and those niggas were still partying. He left them and ended up in front of Anise's house because she was closer than his house and he was drunk and high as fuck. He got out and made his way to the door. He rung her bell and waited for her to answer. Monte knew she was probably gone cuss his ass out for coming this late. She opened the door looking good as hell. His dick instantly stood at attention.

"What the hell are you doing at my door this late Monte?" she asked irritated.

"Ma a nigga fucked up and I need to lay on the couch." She moved to the side and let him in. As bad as she wanted to tell him to leave she couldn't. She cared too much to let him drive home like that.

"Thanks ma." She walked out without a word but came back a few seconds later with a pillow and blanket.

"Thanks baby girl." Monte thanked her.

"You're welcome, " he said, watching her fat ass jiggle as she walked away.

Damn I miss her ass. He thought. He tried to get comfortable on the couch but he couldn't.

"Fuck this shit man." He headed to the room with Anise and climbed right in the bed with her.

"What are you doing Monte?"

"Sshh, let's go to sleep ma." He pulled her in his arms and now he was comfortable. She didn't say anything because she actually like being in his arms again.

Monte had to pee bad as hell but baby girl was laying on him. He didn't want to move her but he had too. All that liquor he had consumed earlier was ready to come out. He slid from up under her and she didn't wake up. He headed to the bathroom to relieve himself. When he came back she was still sleeping and Monte was feeling bold. He climbed back in bed and pushed her boy shorts to the side. Her pink lips were looking nice and edible. He licked it nice and slow. She squirmed but kept her eyes closed. He licked a little faster, biting on her clit just enough to get her going.

"Shit Monte!" she was trying to move away from him but he wasn't having that. He clamped his arms around her legs to keep her in place and went to work.

"Be still ma." Her shit was tasty and he knew that nigga Stone wasn't doing it like him. Call him cocky but he knew how she liked it. Within minutes her legs were shaking and he sucked up every drop. After she had calmed down from her orgasm, Monte climbed up next to her and held her. No words were said. Neither of them knew what to say nor where to go from here. Only time would tell.

This was the third time this week that Lovely had went to bed without her husband and she was fed up with the shit. She didn't know what had gotten into Phalon but this was not him at all. Something had to give. She heard him pull in the garage and looked at the time. It was 3:15.

This nigga got me all the way fucked up.

She sat up in the bed and waited for him to come in the room. It took him a good minute to come in but when he did she lit into that ass.

"You must have lost yo mind coming up in here at this hour!" Lovely yelled.

"Chill ma, a nigga had a long day and I don't need to hear all that shit." She looked at him like he had grew a second head.

"Excuse you. Nigga you got me all the way bent. Aint shit open this late but legs, so where the hell have you been?" Phalon ignored her and walked into the bathroom that was in their room. She got up and went right behind him.

"So you don't hear me Phalon?" He was pissing but still didn't respond. Lovely mushed him in the back of the head. She hated to be ignored and he knew that shit.

"Get the fuck on Lovely, damn. A nigga just told you he had a long day and all you wanna do is fight over nothing!" He shouted with fire in his eyes. It was a look she wasn't familiar with. Something told her to leave it alone but she couldn't go out like a punk bitch.

"Yeah ok nigga, well you might as well go back out the door to that bitch you just left."

"That's how you really feel ma? Huh? A nigga out here busting his ass to take care of his family and all you wanna do is argue and accuse me of some bullshit."

She stood there with her arms folded giving him a look that said she was serious. She wasn't some weak bitch that was gone let a nigga walk all over her.

"Aight ma you got that. You want me to leave then I'm out." Phalon put his clothes back on and walked out the door. She really didn't want him to go but her gut was telling her shit wasn't kosher.

Lovely walked over to the chaise that sat in the corner of their room and curled up on it. She let the tears fall as she thought about what had just happened between her and her husband. *How did we get like this? Maybe I was wrong but I chalk it up to my hormones because this baby had me gone.*

Yes she had found out she was pregnant and hadn't even told Phalon yet. Things went from sugar to shit fast. She could only hope things would get better.

Phalon couldn't believe Lovely accused him of cheating. All he do is work to take care of her and the kids and this was how she treated him. He was too tired to deal with her arguing so he headed to the holiday inn. He needed a good night's rest before dealing with the drama. He laid in bed trying his hardest to let sleep take over but he hadn't been at odds with Lovely since they were married and the shit was eating him up. Something had to give.

Phalon laid there forever before falling asleep but he felt refreshed. He looked at the time on his phone and it read 12:15. He had slept a long time but it was needed. He saw that he had a few missed calls from Kimani, Rahsaan and Anise. He knew what Rahsaan and Anise wanted so he didn't even bother to call them back. This was between him and his wife. He called Kimani back to see what she wanted.

"Hey daddy." She answered.

"What's up baby girl?" He talked to her as he put on his clothes.

"Nothing, you weren't here when we got up so I was just checking on you. And London is calling you." Kimani laughed. Phalon loved his girls and they were both daddy's girls.

"I'm on my way home now baby girl. Where is Lovely?"

"She's in the room. Nana is over here with us because Lovely wasn't feeling good." Damn, he knew he needed to get home before the whole world knew their damn business. He shook his head at how smart and observant his daughter was.

"Ok baby girl, daddy is on the way." He hung up and headed out the door. He needed to fix this shit.

CHAPTER FOUR

"Well I have to get home but I'll call you ok?" Asha looked over at the man lying next to her. She felt like shit because he wasn't her husband but she had just got through getting her back blew out by him. She knew it was wrong but shit happens. She never meant for this to happen because she love Rahsaan but she just wasn't getting the attention she craved from him anymore. All he cared about was the club and record label. All she wanted was some time for her and she couldn't even get that.

"Sure you do. I don't know why you keep going back if you're not happy Asha." Zierre grabbed her from behind and she moved his hands.

"Don't do this Zierre, you know I am married and I love my husband." She said honestly. But did she really love him if she was cheating on him? She needed to get this shit under control and quick because she knew how Rahsaan got down and he wouldn't hesitate to fuck her up.

This was one of the many nights her husband was at the club late. The kids were spending the weekend with Rahsaan's mom so she had snuck out to see Zierre. She had met Zierre a few months back at the grocery store and the chemistry was wild. Don't get it twisted though, she wasn't leaving her husband for him. He was just something to do in her spare time since she had plenty of it.

"Whatever ma, I'm not about to keep being your little secret. It's obvious that with him aint where you want to be otherwise you wouldn't be in my bed."

She watched him walk into the bathroom and close the door. It was going on two in the morning and she had to get home before her husband came home. She didn't even bother saying bye to Zierre because he was in his feelings.

Asha almost shitted bricks when she pulled up. Her husband was actually home for a change and now she had to explain why the hell she was coming in the house close to three am. She sat in the car for a good ten minutes trying to come up with something but she didn't have shit. All the lights were out so Asha was hoping he was sleep. She got out and crept in the house. She took her shoes off downstairs so that she wouldn't make any noise going up the stairs. When she walked in the room his back was turned and he was still. Good he was sleep. She slowly took her clothes off but before she could finish he startled her.

"So that's what you do now, creep in at three in the morning?"

Shit! She was busted and didn't know what the hell to say.

"You don't have shit to say?" Zierre gave her an out.

She was at a lost for words. She had never been so scared in her life. At that moment she knew she had fucked up and didn't know if it could be fixed.

"It's cool ma, at least I know what it is between us. I hope that nigga was worth it." Zierre got up and put on his clothes.

"Where are you going, " Asha asked.

The look he gave her said back off.

Damn what have I done?" She thought.

Never in a million years did Rahsaan think Asha would step out on him but she did. That shit had him fucked up. He had to leave the house to keep from putting his hands on her ass. He felt like choking the shit out of her. Rahsaan headed straight to his mom's house.

It was late so he crept in quietly. He didn't want to wake anyone but this was the only place he could go and get some peace. He didn't need his boys in his business. He laid right on the couch and went to sleep not knowing what was going on with his wife.

Rahsaan woke up to little hands hitting him in the face. It was Romell.

"What's up man?"

Romell just smiled. "Up." He motioned for Rahsaan to pick him up.

Rahsaan sat up and put him on his lap. A few minutes later Brielle walked in the living room.

"Hey daddy." Brielle was a little diva. Darlene had her all dressed up and she was carrying a purse. Rahsaan had to laugh.

"Hey baby." He kissed her cheek and she sat down next to him."

"You slept here last night?" His mom asked as she walked in the room.

"Yeah, but I really don't want to discuss the reason right no, " he said motioning towards the kids. One thing he never wanted was for them to know when their parents were at odds. His mom shook her head in understanding.

"So what do you guys have planned for the day?" He asked his mom.

"We're going to the zoo and then to get ice cream." His mom knew she spoiled her grandkids.

"Well I'm about to head home. I got some things to handle with my wife." Rahsaan stood not really ready to go but he knew it had to be done.

"Ok, well if you want I can keep the kids and extra day, you know I'm lonely over here anyway." She laughed.

"That's fine ma. Love yall." He kissed them all and headed out the door.

<><><><>

When Rahsaan walked in the house Asha was laid out on the couch with a empty Seagram's bottle.

"Really Asha? You drinking that shit now?" He looked at her with disgust. This was not the woman he fell in love with.

Asha strained not to see double. "Look I don't want to fight with you Rah. I fucked up and I understand if you don't want nothing to do with me. Just know that I still love you."

"Look ma, I don't know what made you do what you did but that shit is fucking with me. I have never cheated on you and thought I was doing a damn good job at being a husband, father and provider. If you wasn't happy then you could have said something instead of stepping out on me." He was hurt and that hurt caused him not to even try and work out things with Asha.

"You are a good man Rah, I don't know why I did it but I am sorry. I really am." She pleaded but he was done with it.

"It's cool ma but I'm moving out. You can have the house and all I ask is that I get to see my kids whenever I want. I will still provide for you because I wouldn't be a real man if I didn't." He got up and headed to the bedroom that he shared with his wife. He packed a bag and left just as quick as he had come. He had gone there with every intention of working things out but when he saw her, the thought of her with another man made his decision for him. As he drove to the Holiday Inn he thought about his future with his wife and kids. He honestly didn't know where they were headed. Only time would tell.

CHAPTER FIVE

Lovely and Phalon had been real distant towards each other for the last two weeks and he was tired of it. Phalon felt she was mad at him for nothing. This the type of shit that made a nigga want to cheat. Only thing was, he could never see himself hurting his wife on purpose. Now don't get it twisted because he was still a man and had eyes but he knew how to control his dick. Or at least he thought he did until the day he met Melanie. She came into Epiphany for a waitressing job and she was bad as fuck. Phalon had to think about his kids to keep from having thoughts about her. It's crazy because he's seen plenty of bad chicks since he's been with Lovely and not once did that shit faze him. Phalon knew what he had at home. So why did this chick come up in here and have his dick standing at attention?

"So have you ever waitressed before?" He asked her during the interview.

"Yeah I was a hooter girl for three years."

That shit made him look up at her breast and them bad boys were nice and perky. He estimated her to be about a 36d. "Ok well can you start tomorrow?" Phalon knew he probably shouldn't have hired her but he was thinking with the wrong head. All he could picture was being between her thighs beating it up.

"Yes. Thanks so much. I really appreciate it." She stood and put her hand out and he took hold of her perfectly manicured hand.

Damn her hands are soft and would probably feel good around my dick He thought.

Damn it Pha stop. He knew Lovely would fuck him up if she even thought he was up to no good. Phalon saw Melanie out the door and locked up. He needed to head home to his wife before he fucked up.

When Phalon walked in the house it was quiet which was unusual because London was always running around. He knew Kimani was with Ryan which wasn't unusual. He headed upstairs and found Lovely asleep in their bed with London. He smiled at how cute they were. Phalon walked over and picked London up and took her to her own room. Lovely had a bad habit of letting her sleep in their bed and he had to nip that shit in the bud. When he came back he crawled in bed behind his wife and pulled her close to him. He loved this woman with everything in him. She woke up and looked at him.

"Baby I'm sorry." He kissed her. "You good ma. I'll do better about coming home at a decent hour." He kissed her lips again.

"Bae, I'm pregnant again."

Whoa. Phalon was not expecting that but he was happy. To have her carry his seeds was something he loved. "Word ma?" He had the biggest smile on his face as Lovely nodded her head.

"So that's why you been so damn evil lately." He joked but she didn't find it funny. "I'm joking ma. I love you."

"I love you too bae."

Phalon was horny and it had been almost two weeks since she gave him some so he was about to make up for lost time. He kissed her lips while his hands roamed over her body. Lovely's body was still tight. You would never be able to tell she had given birth before.

She climbed on top of him and took control and Phalon loved that shit. Too bad they didn't get far because London walked in the room. Damn, talk about blocking. Lovely got up to get her.

"What's wrong mama, " Lovely asked as she got off the bed.

"Eat." London said in her barely audible toddler voice.

"Well I guess I'll go cook dinner and get her situated." She looked at me apologetic.

"No worries, when she go to sleep I'm tearing that ass up." He winked at her and headed to the bathroom. He was just happy to be on good terms with her.

Anise hadn't spoken to Monte since he showed up at her door drunk and truth be told she couldn't stop thinking about him. She knew in her heart she wanted to be with him but her head was telling her something different. She had been avoiding Stone too because all he wanted to talk about was them being in a relationship and she wasn't feeling him like that. The sex was off the chain but she didn't share the same feelings that he did.

Anise was laid up watching Netflix in her pajamas. All her girls were all booed up with their husbands and she was the single friend so she stayed clear as much as possible. She didn't want to be the third wheel or make them feel obligated to include her on things. So tonight it was just her, the TV and some snacks. She turned on The Wood, which was one of favorite movies and got comfortable on the couch. Not even ten minutes into the movie, her cell was going off. It was a text from Monte.

Monte: Open the door ma.

This nigga here. She got up and opened the door ready to tell him off for just popping up but he was looking too damn good. She could tell he was high as hell, and his dreads were hanging down. *Damn I loved this nigga with his bow legged ass.*

"What's up ma?" He spoke in a deep Baritone that made her thong soaked.

"Hey." She stepped to the side to let him in. After she closed the door she went back to the couch and sat down trying to keep her mind on the TV and not him.

"So why you in the house on a Friday?" He asked

"Just chilling. Aint really shit too do. All my girls are married and booed up so."

He smiled. "Well can I chill with you ma, " he asked.

"Sure."

He kicked his shoes off and got comfortable. "You love this damn movie."

"Yeah and, " Anise said with a little sarcasm.

"Chill ma." She gave him the side eye and he pulled her in his arms and they just chilled. It was like old times and she liked it.

It was after midnight and Monte was on the couch sleep. He was too damn fine. Anise shook him.

"What's up ma, " he asked never opening his eyes.

"You look tired, go get in the bed." Anise knew she probably should have made him leave but she wanted him there with her.

He looked at her."You sure ma? I can head out, it's late." He responded.

"Nah, you're tired and so am I." Anise got up and grabbed his hand and they headed to her room and he took off his shirt and his pants. *Damn I missed looking at his body.* He climbed in bed and pulled her to him. It felt good to be in his arms, even if only for one night.

"You know I still love you ma and anything you need I got you," he said while kissing her neck.

"I know Monte. I love you too." He kissed her neck again and I let out a soft moan. Her body was on fire. "Monte make love to me." Anise couldn't believe she let that shit come out but there was no turning back now.

<><><><>

Rahsaan wasn't messing with Asha and she had fell into a deep depression. She missed her husband but she had fucked it up. He would come get the kids and drop off some money and just as fast as he came he'd leave. Asha even tried looking sexy for him but it didn't work. She was tainted and he didn't want her anymore. She needed to get out of the house before she went crazy. The only hope that Asha had of them reconciling was his clothes that still hung in their closet.

Asha got up and showered so she could head to Ryan's house. She needed to talk to someone. Ryan was always understanding and never judgmental.

When Asha pulled up Ryan was sitting on the porch watching the twins play.

"Hey girl, " Asha greeted her friend.

"Hey mama. What's going on with you, " Ryan questioned.

"Girl I fucked up."

Ryan gave her a knowing look. She knew that Asha and Rahsaan were beefing but didn't know what it was about.

"So you wanna talk about it?" Ryan asked her.

"I cheated on Rah." Asha could tell by the look on Ryan's face that she wasn't expecting her to say that.

"Damn girl. So what are you doing to fix this? I mean we all make mistakes but you all took vows for better or worse. Don't give up so easily. Even if he's pissed right now give him some time but don't give up without a fight."

"I hear you girl. I just feel like shit. Rah is a good man."

Asha was thankful for Ryan. She was real cool and always there to talk to. She could only hope her husband would come home.

"Don't worry ma, it'll work out. One thing I know about Rah is he loves you. Love trumps all. Just have faith."

Asha wanted to believe that but she was so unsure of what the future held for them.

CHAPTER SIX

Monte was stressed. All Kyah kept talking about was him committing to her or she wasn't going to let him see his daughter. He couldn't deal with it. He needed to relieve this stress. He needed to see Anise. She was the only one who could calm him down. Monte grabbed his keys and headed out the door. He had been texting and talking on the phone with Anise since they slept together a week ago. He was surprised she wanted him stay over, let alone have sex.

When he pulled up to Anise's house there was another car in the driveway but he didn't give a damn. He needed her. Monte knocked on the door and waited. But what he never expected was for that nigga Stone to answer the door.

"What up man, " Stone asked as he blocked the doorway.

"Anise here?" Monte cut straight to the chase.

"Yeah but we were kind of busy." Stone had the nerve to say.

It took everything in Monte not to hit Stone. He knew Anise was wifey and he had crossed the line.

"Look, man, can you go get Anise?"

Before he could respond, Anise yell out. "Stone who's at my door?"

She walked up. "Hey Monte." She smiled.

"What's this ma?" Monte pointed at Stone.

"Oh, Stone came over to talk. Why what's up, Monte, " she asked like nothing was wrong.

"Nothing. Be good ma." He walked away. It was clear that she wanted to be with that nigga so Monte left. He was done chasing Anise. Yeah he loved her and wanted to be with her but he wasn't gone beg her ass either.

Ryan felt bad for Asha but she was wrong in so many ways. Rahsaan trusted her and that's a lot for him because he didn't trust many. Ryan just prayed that they were able to work out their issues. Ryan was having Lunch with Mia, Kita and Yvette today and she had invited Asha, Lovely and Anise. She thought it would be good for them to get away from their everyday life because they knew nothing about what it took to be a hustler's wife.

They met up at Benihana's. Mia and Yvette were already there.

"Hey ladies, it's been a minut, " Ryan greeted as she sat down.

"You looking good girl." Yvette complimented her.

"Thank ya ma'am. So what have you ladies been up too?" Ryan had to catch up with the girls because being a wife and mom left very little time to do so.

"Girl, Harlem and his kids driving me crazy, " Mia joked. She and Harlem were like hood royalty. He was that nigga and she was his wife. Not wifey but wife. So many young girls get the titles confused. They had been through a lot but were able to come out on top.

"Girl bye, they aint shit compared to Tez ass. He keep talking about having more kids. Not I sweetie." Yvette laughed. The waitress came and they ordered drinks and appetizers.

"What's up bitches?!" That was Kita's ghetto self. Nevertheless she was their girl too.

"Hey boo, " Ryan greeted.

"So where are the new wives at?" Kita asked about Lovely, Anise and Asha.

"They should be on the way. They're cool, a little naïve but cool as hell." Ryan told them. She knew how Kita was about new people.

"We have to get together with the kids and do something. Maybe a cookout, " Mia suggested. She was like the Queen bee of the whole crew. Even though Harlem passed the torch to King she was still at the top of the pyramid. They all respected her and loved her.

"We really do, " Kita replied as the other girls walked up.

"Hello Ladies." Asha greeted.

They had met her before because she and Rahsaan had been high school sweethearts.

"Hey Asha girl, it's been a long time, " Mia greeted.

"It has. This is Lovely and Anise. Phalon and Monte's wives." Asha introduced them.

"Uh, I'm Anise and Monte and I aren't together." Anise corrected Asha. Ryan had to laugh because she wasn't fooling no one but herself. They all knew Anise was still in love with Monte.

"Well sounds like trouble in paradise, " Mia said taking a sip of her drink.

"No, we've been broke up well over a year, " Anise informed them.

"Since we're talking about break ups, Mia, why don't you school us on how you and Harlem survived your issues." Ryan asked.

"Well it was far from easy. We dealt with cheating, exes popping up with kids, kidnapping. I mean a lot. But at the end of the day he was my heart. A lot of those things come with being a hustler's wife. You have to have thick skin and be able to handle the drama. A man needs to know that when shit pops off that his girl is there. Will he cheat? Hell yeah, he's a man. You can do everything right and have the best pussy in the world but that aint gone stop that nigga from straying. You have to be able to handle that shit. Not saying it's ok, cause if he fooling around get in his ass." She high fived Kita.

"Our men deal with enough in these streets so when they come home, they want to be at peace. Just have their backs and the rest will fall in place. But don't be dumb either and let them get a pass on that shit either." Mia schooled her friends..

"I hear you girl, because I know King and I have had our share of drama." They laughed.

"Well we definitely have to do this more often. I know it's stressful dealing with these knuckleheads but we're the wives of hustlers." Yvette laughed.

"Well to new friendships." Mia toasted. This was definitely a new beginning to their sisterhood.

CHAPTER SEVEN

Asha was cooking dinner while Romell and Brielle watched Disney channel. It had been three months since Rahsaan had moved out and she was dealing with it better than she thought. Asha had cut all ties with Zierre but he was still calling and harassing her.

She heard Brielle yell *Daddy* which mean he was here. Weird because it wasn't the weekend. Asha continued to cook.

"Mommy daddy's here." Brielle walked in the kitchen holding Rah's hand.

"I see baby. Go wash your hands so you can eat mama." Asha told Brielle as she ran to the bathroom.

"Hey Rah." Asha spoke.

"What's up?" He sat down at the kitchen table.

"Just getting dinner ready so they can take their baths and go to bed. They have been driving me crazy all day." She laughed.

"Oh yeah, I know Brielle is a mess. So have you decided what you want to do for her birthday?' Brielle was turning three in a few months.

"Not really, maybe we can just have a cookout." Asha suggested.

"That's cool. We can get Dora and Hello Kitty. That would be dope since she likes them."

"Ok cool, " Asha agreed.

Asha and Rahsaan hadn't had a decent conversation in quite some time but it felt good.

"Well let me go kick it with my lil' man before I head out." He got up and Asha felt a tear fall. She hated that he had to leave. She hated that they were no longer together. But it is what it is. Asha knew it was time to move on. Her husband was through with her and she had to accept that. A few minutes later Rah walked back in with Romell. He put him in his highchair and then called Brielle. She came running in. Asha fixed their plates and got them situated. It was an awkward silence in the room.

"Did you want me to fix you a plate?" She asked to break the silence.

"Nah, I gotta get out of here, but I'll be by tomorrow to get them, " he said as he got up. He kissed the kids and left. This shit was for the birds.

After the kids ate Asha gave them a bath and put them to bed. She was so used to her husband being there and now that he wasn't she rarely slept. She would sleep maybe three hours a night. Something had to give.

<><><><>

Rahsaan loved his wife but he couldn't be with her; at least not right now. Every time he was in her presence he thought about her being with another man. That shit was really fucking with him because he hated being away from his kids. He had stopped by Snookers to grab a drink. Rahsaan was on his second Long Island when he saw his ex, Tracy. They had kicked it for a good year and he had feelings for her but he wasn't in love with her. He was more in love with the pussy. She was a good girl though. She still looked good too. Rahsaan headed over to her table and saw she was with Chrissy and Tamika.

"What's up ladies? It's been a while."

"Hey Rahsaan!" Tracy hugged him. *Damn she felt good in my arms.*

"Hey Rah." Chrissy and Tamika spoke. Chrissy was Javon's side piece but once he and Trina were back on good terms he stopped messing with Chrissy. They still kicked it with Ryan but they barely came around.

"So what's been up with yall, " Rahsaan asked.

"Aint shit, you know I moved to Lansing so I'm only down here for a few days, " Tracy responded.

"Awe damn ma, Rah said. Ok well make some time for ya boy."

She gave him the side eye. "Where is Asha?"

Damn did everybody and their mama know about her? He thought. "At her house, right now and that ain't nothing to worry about, I guarantee you."

"Ooh is there trouble in paradise?" She teased.

"Man chill. You hanging with me or not?" Rah waited.

Tracy smiled and then looked at her girls. "I guess I'll see you ladies later." After downing her drink she grabbed his hand and they headed out.

"Ooh shit Rah that's my spot!" Rahsaan was blowing Tracy's back out. Her fat ass was jiggling every time he went in from the back. One thing he did remember about Tracy was that she was good in bed.

"You like that shit ma?" He was still pissed at Asha and taking it out on Tracy's pussy. But she liked that rough sex.

"Ye. Fuck me Rah!" Her wish was his command. He didn't feel an ounce of regret. The way he saw it, his wife had been fucking another nigga for god knows how long. Plus they weren't together and probably never would be.

"Shit Rah I'm cumming!." That was all it took for him to bust. He pulled out of her and slid the condom off. He went to the bathroom to dispose of it.

"I see you still a beast in the bed nigga, " Tracy said when he came back in the room.

"Well you know." Rahsaan joked as he laid down next to her.

"So what's the deal with wifey? I mean you living in your own apartment and everything. Is it that bad?" Tracy was someone Rahsaan cared about and he could always talk to so he felt comfortable confiding in her.

"She cheated. Everything I did for her and she stepped out on me. I don't know if that's something I can forgive man." He shook his head at the thought.

"Well I don't know Asha but I know you and you're a good man Rah. If you love her work it out. But if it doesn't work know that I'll be here to pick up the pieces. I mean we didn't end on bad terms but I knew you were in love with her. But it's obvious that she doesn't know what she has at home." Tracy was a good girlfriend when they were together but he just wasn't in love with her so he let her go. Something he now regretted because look where that got him. Rahsaan pulled her close to him and kissed her neck.

"Let's get some sleep ma." He didn't want to talk about Asha anymore. That was a dead issue right now.

Chapter eight

Asha couldn't believe her husband was sitting there laughing and giggling with his ex. Yeah Asha knew all about her and now here he was like they were a happy couple. She couldn't believe this shit. She knew then that it was over. Asha saw how he looked at her. It was the same way that he used to look at her. Asha's heart was broken in two and it was her own fault. She gathered her things and left the restaurant. She was supposed to be meeting Ryan for lunch but after that she didn't have an appetite. Asha sent Ryan a text to let her know something came up. She went straight to the city county building.

Asha walked in with her head held high even though she felt like shit.

"Next in line please." The clerk called out. Asha walked up to the counter and tried her best not to break down.

"Yes, I need to file for divorce."

The clerk handed Asha some papers to fill out and she did. She then told her to have a seat and wait for her name to be called. Asha really couldn't believe it had come to this but it was what it was. After waiting thirty minutes her name was called and the clerk gave her some documents and explained to Asha the next steps. Rahsaan would be served his papers and the process would be started.

Asha walked out of the building and broke down. She tried to be strong and not let this break her but it was hard. She really did love her husband and didn't know why she cheated. If she could turn back the hands of time she would. Asha headed home, to an empty house. Darlene had the kids for the weekend so it was just her. Asha knew that she was eventually leaving Detroit once again. That seemed to be an issue she had. Instead of dealing with her problems head on she ran. She couldn't bear to be in the same state as Rahsaan and watch him with another woman. Asha prayed for better days.

Asha woke up to someone knocking on the door. It was probably Rahsaan since she had changed the locks on his ass. He had a new house and a new bitch so he didn't need access to her house. She went to door and opened it.

"Why the hell you change the locks?" Rah looked at her like she had two heads.

"You don't live here therefore you don't need access to my house." Asha walked away.

"Have you lost ya damn mind? I pay the bills here not you, he barked.

"Nigga please. You laid up with yo new bitch so miss me with that bullshit."

"You funny as hell. You so worried about me being laid up with someone else when it could have been you had you kept ya legs closed. But it's cool ma. I hope you can afford to keep this place since I don't have any rights here as you say then I won't be paying the bills."

"I don't care Rah. You forgot you didn't marry no hoodrat ass bitch! Nigga I got money, I don't need ya money. Fuck you and that bitch!" He walked out the door without any words. Asha was tired; emotionally and physically. She was getting her babies and going back to Atlanta. Asha was done with men. All she wanted was to be alone with her kids. She called Darlene and told her to get the kids ready because she was picking them up today. She didn't need this house or nothing in it.

Asha got dressed and packed the kids a bag for the road. Once she was done she headed to pick them up.

"Hey Asha is everything ok?" Darlene asked her when she opened the opened the door.

"Yeah I just want to spend some time with my kids, " she lied. Asha didn't need her knowing her business so she could tell Rahsaan that she was leaving.

"Ok well let me know if you need anything Asha." Darlene was concerned.

She gathered the kids and put them in the car and they were on their way.

Asha decided to drive to Atlanta because she knew Rahsaan would find her if she flew. She had no intentions on keeping him from his kids but she needed to get settled in before she told him where they were. Asha knew that he would try to make her stay and that was something she just couldn't do. She needed to get over him and the best way would to be away from him.

"Mommy I want my daddy, " Brielle cried. She was really a daddy's girl.

"We're going to call him soon ok baby." Asha felt bad that they were leaving behind the only family they knew but she felt this was something she had to do.

"Ok mommy." her voice broke Asha's heart but she kept driving. She was four hours into the drive when Rahsaan called. Asha didn't answer. She wasn't ready to talk to him just yet.

After what seemed like forever Asha was entering the Georgia state line. She didn't know what she was going to do as of yet but she was ready to start this new journey with her kids.

<><><><>

Rahsaan had been blowing Asha's phone up and she wasn't answering. His mom told him that she picked the kids up but she wasn't at home either. Something told him shit wasn't kosher but he didn't know what was going on. Rahsaan tried calling her again. The phone rang three times before she finally picked up.

"Hello?" She answered like nothing was wrong. Rahsaan wanted to choke the shit out of her ass.

"Where the hell are you with my kids, " he questioned..

"First off, watch how you talk to me. Second, don't worry we're fine." Asha was really pushing his buttons.

"Asha, I'm coming to get my kids so have yo ass at home."

"I can't do that Rah, " she said in a nonchalant attitude. He tried his hardest to keep calm.

"What's the deal Asha? I just want to see my kids."

"Rah, I'm not in Detroit anymore. Once I get settled we'll work something out with you seeing the kids."

"Are you fucking kidding me! Where the hell are my kids Asha? Yo ass playing games and you know how I roll." He was beyond pissed.

"I'm in Atlanta."

Rahsaan couldn't believe she took his kids to Atlanta. The same place where she almost died. They still hadn't found Alana and Rahsaan didn't feel comfortable with her taking his kids to Atlanta. "Really Asha?" He hung up the phone. Rahsaan couldn't believe she would take his kids away from him. He didn't do shit to her ass. She was the one that cheated not him. Words couldn't even describe how he felt right now.

<><><><>

Asha had been gone for almost two weeks. Rahsaan missed his kids dearly and had only spoke to them on the phone. That wasn't enough. A knock at the door brought him out of his thoughts. When he opened the door it was a short, gray haired white man.

"Can I help you"

"Yes. Are you Mr. Rahsaan Johnson?"

"I am."

He passed Rahsaan an envelope. "You've been served." He walked away just as quickly as he came.

CHAPTER NINE

Anise haven't seen Monte in almost two months.
She's been avoiding his ass like the plague. She was
sitting in the bathroom waiting for the results of the
pregnancy test she'd just taken. Her nerves were shot.
All these years she had practiced safe sex and the one
time she slipped with Monte she gets pregnant. Either
that or she had a bug for over a damn month. She knew
better without even looking at the test. After waiting
long enough she finally looked at the test and sure
enough she was pregnant. She didn't know what her
next step was. Hell, she wasn't even with the father. She
didn't know whether or not she was going to keep it. She
had a lot to think about and she needed her best friend
right now. She picked up her cell phone and called
Lovely.

"Hello?' Phalon answered Lovely's phone.

"Hey Pha, is Lovely around?"

"She sleep sis. I'll tell her to call you when she
wakes up."

Damn. "Ok." She hung up and was back to
feeling alone. She decided to call Ryan because she knew
she wouldn't judge her. She had to tell somebody and
she wasn't ready to tell Monte. That would be all he
needed to try and get back with her.

"Hello?"

"Hey Ry are you busy?"

"Not at all. What's up?"

"Girl, I just took a pregnancy test and it came back positive."

"Oh. So did you tell Stone?" *How the hell did everybody know I was fucking him?* She thought.

"Damn was it that obvious that we were fucking?"

"Bitch, yes."

"Damn. But it's not his. It's Monte's"

"Oh snap!. When the hell did y'all get back together?"

"We aren't. He came by one night and we slept together, without a condom."

"Girl you in some deep shit there. So you are keeping it right?"

"I'm not sure. I'm confused and I don't want to be a baby mama." The tears that she was holding back finally made their way down her face.

"Aww don't cry. One thing I can tell you is that Monte loves you girl. He will be there for you. But please tell that man he has a baby on the way. It's only fair that you all make the decision together. But no matter what you know I'm here for you." Ryan felt bad for her. She was in a messed up situation. She knew all too well how it felt not to trust the one you love.

"Thanks Ry. I'm going to take a nap. This shit is stressing me out."

"No problem mama. Get some rest and I'll be over later to check on you."

Anise hung up feeling a little better. She needed a nap befor

e she could deal with this any further. She knew that shit was about to get real complicated.

<><><><>

Brielle's birthday was approaching and Asha knew she had to go back to Detroit. She wouldn't dare keep Rahsaan away from his kids. She just had to get things in order for herself. She found a three bedroom Condo and had a few job interviews lined up. Asha called Ryan to let her know that she was coming back for Brielle's birthday. She wanted to do it at her house.

"Hello, " Ryan answered.

"Hey Ry."

"You know I'm about to cuss yo ass out right?" Asha knew that was coming. She hadn't told anyone she was moving. Mainly because she didn't want Rahsaan to find out and stop her.

"I know. Don't be mad at me Ry. I had to do what was needed for me. But I'm coming back next week for Brielle's birthday. So can you get everything together for me? I would love to have it at your house. Just the family."

"Girl you know I got you. We miss y'all. And that nigga Rah going crazy without you ma."

"Bitch please. I can't tell the way he was flaunting his ex around."

"He was hurt Asha. Trust me Tracy is no one. I know because that's my girl but her and Rah are no good together."

"Well I really don't want to talk about that right now. But I'll be flying in Thursday so can you pick me up?" Asha asked. She was nervous about returning but it was Brielle's birthday so she had to put her feelings aside.

"Of course. What time does your plane land?" Ryan asked. She was happy that Asha and the kids were coming back. She just hoped Rahsaan didn't act a fool.

"Noon, " Asha responded.

"Ok, I'll be there. I can't wait to see you and my babies."

"We miss you too sis. Well let me get the kids ready for bed and I'll see you soon." Asha hung up. She didn't know what to expect when she saw Rahsaan but she knew she had to face him sooner or later. She just hoped he wasn't too mad.

Chapter Ten

Ryan had told Rahsaan that Asha and the kids were coming back. She knew Asha didn't tell him but Ryan felt loyalty to Rahsaan even though Asha was her girl. Rahsaan told Ryan he'd pick them up from the airport and Ryan agreed only if he promised not to act a fool. He agreed. All he wanted was to see his kids.

It was Thursday afternoon and Rahsaan was waiting at the airport for Asha and the kids. He spotted them by baggage claim and walked over. Even though he talked to them on the phone, he hadn't seen his kids in a month.

"Daddy's baby, " He called out, causing Brielle to turn around. She ran to him and that made his heart melt.

"Daddy!" He picked her up and hugged her tight. Asha turned around with a sleeping Romell in her arms. Rahsaan put Brielle down and walked over to Asha.

"Let me take him." He grabbed Romell out of her arms. He pulled Asha in for a hug which surprised her. Rahsaan was ready to put the issues they had behind them. They had two children to raise so they needed to get along.

"Come on y'all." Rahsaan led the way to his car. When they got there he buckled in Romell, who was still sleeping in his car seat and Brielle buckled herself. After making sure everybody was good, Rahsaan headed home, the home he once shared with his family.

The whole ride Asha was quiet. The only conversation was between Rahsaan and Brielle. Asha felt awkward in his presence. When they pulled up to the house Asha was the first to get out. She had planned to stay at Ryan's but it seemed Rahsaan had other plans for them so she just kept quiet.

"Go ahead inside and I'll grab y'all bags." He threw Asha the keys. Because she had the locks changed before she left, he had to have them changed again. He still had his apartment but he kept the house up for her just in case she decided to come back.

Brielle went straight to her room. Asha looked around and saw that everything was the same way she had left it. She could tell Rahsaan cleaned up because everything was neat and in place.

"Here's your bags. I'm going to take them to see my mom. You wanna ride?" He was hoping she said yes. Even though they were separated and damn near headed for divorce, Rahsaan missed her. It took for her and the kids to leave for him to realize that he forgave her.

"Um, no. Y'all can go ahead. I'm going to get situated."

Rahsaan looked at her and saw the Asha he fell in love with. "Alright I'll have them back before bedtime." Romell was now awake and reaching for Rahsaan. Asha felt bad because they had really missed their dad. "Ok." Rahsaan called Brielle downstairs and they headed out the door.

<><><><>

Rahsaan walked in his mom's house with the kids and Darlen's face lit up. She loved her grandbabies and was happy to see them.

"Granny's babies! I missed you guys so much!" She hugged both Brielle and Romell.

"Can I please keep them for the night?" She asked Rahsaan.

"Let me call and see if Asha had any plans." Rahsaan pulled out his phone and called her.

"Hello?" She answered.

"Hey mama wanted to keep the kids tonight. Is that cool?"

"Sure."

"Alright cool. You need anything ma?" He asked her.

"Nah, I'm good. I'm going to order some food and chill since they aren't coming back tonight."

Rahsaan wanted to go back to the house with her but he didn't know if it was a good idea.

"Alright then. Call me if you need anything." He hung up and Darlene was staring at him.

"What?" he asked.

"You still love that girl. Fix this shit, Rah. I know what she did but love trumps all. Don't let one mistake fuck up y'all marriage. You love each other and you all have these babies, "she said before walking away.

"Come on Bri, " she called after her grandaughter. Romell was still glued to his father. Rahsaan knew his mom was right and he was going to make this thing right with his wife.

Tracy had been texting Rahsaan all day and he had yet to respond. She didn't know what was up with him but she wasn't the one. She wasn't into chasing no man. They had become pretty close since Asha was out of the picture and if Tracy had her way, Asha would stay out of the picture. She had let Rahsaan go once and she wasn't about to let him go again. He was a good man but Asha didn't appreciate that.

She decided to call him again. This time he answered.

"What's up, " he answered.

"So, you ain't fucking with me today? I mean I been texting you and you aint respond not once."

Rahsaan sighed. This was what he didn't want. He didn't deal with that with Asha and he wasn't about to deal with it from Tracy. "Man Tracy gone with that shit. First off, we aint together. We just fucking. Second, I was chilling with my kids."

"Oh so yo wife is back. That's why you been ignoring me. It's cool Rah. Just know that I'm not giving you up this time. Fuck her!" Tracy hung up the phone and Rahsaan just shook his head. Something told him Tracy was going to be a problem. He had to take care of that before shit got out of hand.

Since the kids were staying with his mom for the night, he decided to go over to the house and talk to Asha. He knew things wouldn't be the same overnight but he needed to try and make it right. The whole ride to the house Rahsaan contemplated what he was going to say to her. He didn't know if she was seeing anybody or if she was still willing to work things out but he had faith.

When he pulled up to the house all the lights were out. It was after nine and he didn't know if she was sleep or not. He killed the engine and headed inside. He found Asha sleep in their bedroom. She looked so peaceful and innocent. That was his heart and no matter how he tried to get over her he couldn't. She was imprinted on his heart.

Rahsaan climbed in bed behind her and pulled her to him. He missed her and everything about her; her smell; the way she felt in his arms; being deep inside her. He had to get her back. Asha didn't wake up so he just closed his eyes and enjoyed the moment.

Chapter Eleven

Marco had been following Lovely for the last few weeks. He didn't like the fact that she had moved on. She belonged to him and he wasn't about to let her live happily ever after with Phalon. He was obsessed with Lovely and had to have her. He watched her come out of the store. She was finally alone and he was ready to make his move. He got out of the car and walked towards her. As he got closer, he noticed her small but protruding belly. He was pissed. Here she was yet again having a baby by Phalon. He couldn't understand how she was playing house with the next nigga when they had history.

"What's up lady bug?"

Lovely froze. She knew that voice and hated it. Marco had taken her through so much. "What do you want Marco?" She asked without turning around.

"Damn lady bug, it's like that? I thought what we had was special." He walked closer. He was so close that she felt his breath on her neck.

"Are you fucking serious?" She turned to face him. "Leave me alone." She tried to get in her car but Marco grabbed her and threw her against the car. He grabbed her neck.

"Listen to me bitch! You belong to me, always have. You have a week to end things with that nigga and come home or it'll be hell to pay."

Lovely was scared to death. She knew how dangerous Marco was and here she was alone with him. He licked the side of her face before letting her go and walking away. Lovely knew she had to call Phalon. She was so shook up that she could barely dial the number. When she finally dialed it he answered on the first ring.

"What's up bae?" He answered.

"He won't....leave me alone." She stuttered.

Phalon didn't know what she was talking about but he was pissed that somebody was messing with his wife. "Where are you?"

She was so shook up she didn't say anything.

"Hold on bae, I'm going to look at the family locator." Phalon looked up Lovely's location on his cell phone and saw that she was at the grocery store.

"I'm on my way bae. Stay on the phone with me until I get there." Phalon got to the store in no time.

Phalon pulled up beside her car and jumped out leaving the car running. He opened her door and pulled her to him. "What happened?"

She was finally calm enough to explain what happened and Phalon was pissed. He pulled her back and looked at her neck. She had hand prints around her neck and that pissed him off even more.

"Come on ma so I can get you home. I'll have somebody come get ya car." He put her in his car and made a phone call for someone to pick hers up. Lovely knew shit was about to get real. She knew how Marco was but she also knew how her husband rolled.

"So what are the plans for her birthday?" Rahsaan was sitting at the kitchen table while Asha cooked breakfast. He knew that they had discussed the plans before she left but he figured that her plans had changed. They had yet to discuss their issues but they were getting along.

"I was thinking just a small gathering with the family. Nothing too big, " Asha responded with her back still to Rahsaan.

He got up and walked over to her. He placed his hands on her hips and turned her to face him. He just stared at her for a minute and that made Asha nervous. He kissed her lips. At first it was a small peck then he went for some tongue action. To his surprise Asha opened up her mouth and let him kiss her. She put her arms around his neck and he let his hands roam her body. They hadn't been intimate in quite some time. Rahsaan reached around her and turned the stove off before picking Asha up and taking her upstairs.

Rahsaan laid her on the bed and undressed her slowly. Her body was still perfect. Looking at her made him realize how much he missed her. He undressed himself and climbed onto the bed with her.

He kissed her lips and then her breast. Asha laid there anticipating what was to come. Usually Rahsaan loved the chance to feast on her pussy but he was ready to fell the inside of her. It had been too long. He inserted himself in her and Asha gasped.

"You ok?" he asked. She just shook her head and he started moving in and out of her. He was hitting spots she had forgot she had.

"Ooh Rah!" She scratched his back with her nails. That drove him crazy and he started going in.

"Shit bae, this pussy tight as fuck!" Rahsaan was on the verge of cumming.

"Shit Rah I'm cumming!" Her legs shook.

"Me too bae." He let off a load of semen inside her before lying next to her. He pulled her in his arms and kissed her.

Asha laid there for about ten minutes. She was in deep thought about what just happened between them.

"Rah." She called out.

"Whats up ma?" He was still holding on to her.

"What was this? I mean where do we go from here?" Asha didn't want to read too much into it but she wasn't his booty call either.

"Well, you are still my wife and I love you. Let's just take it one day at a time. That is, if you want to, " he replied and that answer was good enough for her.

"Well you know I live in Atlanta."

Rah knew that was coming. "Look we'll cross that bridge when we get there." Rahsaan just wanted his family back and was prepared to do whatever it took to make it happen.

Anise had just come from the doctor and found out she was almost two months pregnant. She still hadn't talked to Monte. He hadn't called her and she didn't want to call him. She knew that she was keeping her baby. She just didn't know how she was going to handle being a single parent. She hadn't even told Lovely. Lovely seemed to be dealing with her own pregnancy and she didn't want to take away from that. She was happy for her girl and hoped to one day have that.

Anise sat with the phone in her hand. She had sat on the couch contemplating for the last hour on how to tell Monte. She knew she had to talk to him before she got too far in her term. She dialed his number. It rang three times before he answered.

"Yo." He answered in that deep baritone that made Anise weak.

"Hey Monte, are you busy, " she asked.

"Naw, just chilling with Aniya, " he said referring to his daughter.

"Well, I need to talk to you when you get the time. It's important."

Monte wondered what was so important that she needed to see him. "Alright. Give me a about an hour. I have to drop her off to her mama."

They hung up and Anise had butterflies. She didn't know how this conversation was going to go but it had to be done.

An hour later Monte was sitting on Anise's couch. He had Aniya with him because he couldn't get in touch with Kyah. That had been happening a lot lately. He didn't know what was up with her but he didn't mind spending time with his daughter.

"So what's up Anise." He went straight in.

"Well, I found out I'm pregnant."

Monte was shocked. He didn't expect to hear her say that at all.

"So who's is it, " he asked because he knew she was fucking him and Stone.

"It's yours. I had stopped sleeping with Stone a while ago plus he always strapped up. You ran in me raw remember Unless you forgot." She replied.

"No offense baby girl, I just need to be sure. So what are your plans? I mean are you keeping it, " he asked as Aniyah began to fuss.

"Of course! " Anise watched him try and calm Aniyah down but it wasn't working. As much as she despised him for cheating, she couldn't deny how cute his daughter was.

"Here let me see her." Anise grabbed Aniyah from him. She put Aniyah across her shoulder and patted her back. She stopped crying. At that moment Anise knew she couldn't wait until her baby was here. Monte watched as Anise put his daughter to sleep.

"Come here ma." He patted the seat next to him and she walked over and sat down with Aniyah still in her arms.

"You know I love you and I'm here for you and my child." He kissed her forehead and reached for Aniyah but Anise pulled away. She actually like holding her. She knew that if she wanted to work things out with Monte, then she had to accept his child.

"I know you will. Can you stay with me tonight, " she asked.

That shocked Monte. "I have to drop her off but I can come back." He stood up and grabbed Aniyah from Anise. He pulled her in his arms.

"I'll be back ma." He headed out the door to drop Aniyah back off to her mom.

Chapter Twelve

Stone was leaning over the coffee table snorting lines of coke. He didn't think he was addicted because he didn't do it often but it made sex great. Right now he had a bad ass stripper from Ace of Spades ready to do whatever.

"Come suck my dick." He laid back and watched the stripper that went by the name of Peaches reach for his dick. She was a pro at what she did and he was horny. While she took him in her mouth he pictured Anise. She was all he seem to think about lately. He couldn't understand how she was so hung up over Monte. The nigga cheated and had a baby on her yet she was still fucking with him. Stone was a good nigga and wanted to give her the world but she was acting funny.

"Yeah suck that shit." He held on to the back of her head and fucked her mouth. Before he knew it he was shooting his seeds down her throat. He felt relief for a moment but he knew it wouldn't last long. He needed and wanted Anise and was willing to do whatever he had to get her. Even kill.

<><><><>

Asha was getting everything ready for Brielle's party. She was ready for it to be over already. She wasn't in the mood for everyone asking about her and Rahsaan splitting up. . She was actually embarrassed because she thought they knew she had cheated. Truth was none of their family knew but Ryan and that was because she told her. Rahsaan didn't believe in having his family in his business.

"Romell sit down in your chair." Asha was trying to decorate the backyard and he was running around. She looked back at him and he still hadn't sat down.

"Mell you heard mommy." Brielle was bossy. She chased after her little brother but he was giving her a hard time. Rahsaan came out to see if Asha needed help and he saw Brielle chasing Romell.

"Daddy, mommy told Mell to sit and he not listening." Brielle told her dad.

"Romell sit, now, " Rahsaan said with authority and that was all it took for Romell to sit. He tested Asha but he knew his dad didn't play.

"Thanks Rah. I've been fussing at that boy all morning."

"You need help?" He asked as he walked over to where she was hanging balloons.

"Nah, just keep him occupied."

"Well I'm about to head out to the barbershop so I'll take him with me. Call me if you need anything." He kissed her cheek and grabbed Romell.

"Come on son." Asha loved how he was with their kids. He was such a great father and husband. She couldn't believe she had messed that up. Even though she seemed to be getting a second chance, she wasn't so sure it would work this time. Too much damage had been done.

"Ok come on Bri, let's get you dressed." Asha had put up the last balloon and everything was ready. She had to get Brielle dressed and wait for the family to arrive. Asha took Brielle into the house and got her dressed. She wore a pink Roc A Wear outfit with pink and grey Nikes. Asha pulled her curly hair into a ponytail and tied it with a ribbon.

"Ok let me put on your earrings." She got up and grabbed the diamond studs that Rahsaan had bought Brielle last Christmas. She put them in her ear.

"Ok, you're all ready."

"Can I look in the mirror mommy?" She was a diva.

"Yeah, come on." Asha picked her up so she could look at her self in the mirror.

"Ok, let's go outside and wait for everyone to get here." They headed outside at the same time Ryan and King were walking in the backyard.

"Hey y'all."

"Hey sis. Hey Bri boo." King picked Brielle up.

"Hi uncle King." King put her down and took her gifts to the table that was designated for them.

"So what time is everyone supposed to be here?" Ryan asked Asha.

"I told them three and it's a quarter till so they should be here soon, " Asha said as she watched Brielle and Chasity play. Those two were thick as thieves right along with London.

"So what's the deal with you and Rah? I mean the plan was for you and the kids to stay with us until you left but I aint heard from yo ass." Ryan laughed.

"Well he wanted us to stay here so I didn't argue with that. Plus he needs to spend as much time with the kids as possible before we head back out." Asha replied.

"Girl bye, you really think he letting yo ass go back to Atlanta?" They laughed as Anise walked up with Aniyah in her arms. That surprised both Asha and Ryan. Every since Anise told Monte that she was pregnant they had been chilling together with Amiyah. Monte hadn't been able to get in touch with Kyah until yesterday and she told him she didn't care what he did with Amiyah. If he wasn't going to be with her than she didn't want their daughter. Monte couldn't believe her but he was willing to take full responsibility for his daughter. It was a plus that Anise was willing to help him. She had taken to Aniyah as if she was the biological mother.

"What y'all laughing at?"

"Yo ass playing step mama." Ryan joked.

"Fuck you." Anise sat down next to the girls. "So what's been going on Asha?" She hadn't seen Asha since before she left.

"Nothing much. Ready for this party to be over already. I am beyond tired but I want Bri to have a good time. I hear that. Lovely and Pha are on their wa, " Asha replied.

"Ok cool."

"So how did this happen?" Ryan asked Anise while pointing to Aniyah.

"Long story girl. Just know her mama trife, " Anise responded.

"Well she seems to be taking to you quite well."

"Yeah, I have fallen in love with this little girl. I cant wait until my baby gets here."

Asha turned her head so fast. "You're pregnant?" Asha asked Anise.

"Yeah. A little over two months."

"By who?"

"Monte."

"Alright nah. Get it." They all laughed as Monte joined them.

"You want me to take her, " he asked. He didn't want Anise to feel uncomfortable with his daughter but she seemed to love having her.

"No, I got her." She smiled and that was why he loved her. He walked away to kick it with King and Harlem who had just walked in the backyard.

"You and Mia are good because aint no way King gone have another child and I be playing mama. Hell no. I will kill his ass." Ryan was serious.

"We know with yo mean ass." Asha replied.

"Hey, I'm just saying, " Ryan replied.

"Whats up ladies, " Mia greeted.

"Hey mama, you looking good there." Ryan admired.

"Thank ya. So what yall over here gossiping about, " Mia asked.

"Me and Rah, you and Anise playing step mama amongst other shit." Asha joked.

"Well who is this cutie?" Mia reached for Aniyah who clung to Anise.

"This is Monte's daughter."

"She sure is attached to you, " Mia observed.

"Yeah I know, " Asha replied. The ladies talked and chilled until everyone arrived and the kids played and had a good time.

It was after seven and the kids had partied and ate cake and ice cream until it was gone. They were now upstairs playing while the adults were downstairs chilling.

"Well I'm going to get on out of here. I have a church meeting in the morning, " Darlene said as she stood up.

"Ok ma. Call me when you get home." Rahsaan walked her to the door before walking back in the living room. He walked over to Asha and pulled her up and sat down before pulling her on his lap.

"Awww, " Mia and Ryan both said.

Rich Boy Mafia 4

"Man shut the hell up, " He replied.

"You shut up fool." Ryan threw a pillow at him. She was happy to see Asha and Rahsaan getting along.

"Well as much as we enjoyed ourselves it's time to get Aniyah home. It's her bedtime." Monte stood up and headed up the stairs to get his daughter. When he came back Anise already had her bag in her hand.

"See y'all later." They headed out.

By ten everyone had left and Asha was cleaning up.

"I'm going to make sure that they are in the bed and then I'll come help you." Rahsaan told Asha as he headed up the stairs. He saw that Romell was in his bed sleep. When he got to Brielle's room she was passed out on the floor. He picked her up and laid her in the bed. After he got her pajamas out he changed her and covered her up. He was happy to have them back and prayed that Asha didn't go back to Atlanta.

Chapter Thirteen

Lovely was approaching her fourth month and sicker than ever. She couldn't hold anything down and she had no energy whatsoever. She looked at her phone and saw that it was almost eight pm. Phalon was supposed to have been home an hour ago. At least that's what he had said. Lovely was thankful for Ryan taking the girls because she didn't have the energy to run behind London.

Just as she was getting comfortable her text notifications went off. She reached over and grabbed the phone.

"What the hell?" She sat up and read the text again because she thought she was tripping. It was a picture of a female ass naked sitting on her husband's desk. Lovely was beyond pissed.

"This nigga done fucked with the wrong one." Lovely got out the bed and headed to her closet but before she could even grab her clothes she heard the door open. A few minutes later Phalon walked in.

"Hey bae. How are you feeling, " he asked. Lovely's response was a Red Bottom to his head.

"What the fuck?" He looked at her like he wanted to beat the shit out of her.

"Fuck you nigga! No wonder yo ass can't come home on time because you too busy fucking these nasty hoes." Phalon was beyond confused and thought her hormones had her acting crazy.

"Baby calm down. What the hell are you talking about?"

"Don't play with me Phalon." She grabbed the phone and tossed it at him. When he saw what was on her phone he became enraged. He knew Melanie was going to be a problem but this shit was going too far.

"Baby I can explain."

SMACK!

"Look, I don't know what the hell is going on but stop putting your hands on me!" He was pissed and Lovely wasn't making it better.

"Get the fuck out! I'm so done with yo ass!"

Phalon knew that it was pointless trying to talk to her right now so he picked up his keys and headed out the door. He was ready to kill Melanie.

Anise was starting to feel happy about her pregnancy. She actually had someone growing inside of her and she couldn't wait to meet her baby. She saw how Monte was with Aniyah and knew that he'd be a good father to their baby.

Anise was chilling today. The further she got in her pregnancy the less she wanted to do. All she wanted was to lay up and get her feet rubbed and Monte happily did it. He wanted it to be as smooth as possible for her.

Anise was comfortable on the couch watching Netflix when the doorbell rang. After pausing her show she went to open the door. It was Monte and Aniyah.

"Hey sweetie." She grabbed Aniyah out of Monte's arms.

"Well damn all you see is her?"

Anise laughed. "Don't be J." She walked away and he followed, watching her ass jiggle.

"Here you go bae." He had brought her Chinese food.

"Awe you do love me." She smiled.

"You know I do. So what you been doing all day?"

"Just relaxing. I missed her so much." She kissed Aniyah's cheeks. Monte loved how Anise took to his daughter. Especially since she was the product of his infidelity.

"Well she must have missed you too because I couldn't get her to go to sleep at all last night. We were up till about 1am."

"Aww. You should have called me. How about you guys stay over here tonight?"

Monte looked at her like she was crazy. They still hadn't defined what they were. They had only slept together that one time, resulting in her getting pregnant.

"I don't think that's a good idea." As much as he wanted to stay he wasn't about to play his self. He wanted to be with Anise but she obviously didn't know what she wanted.

"Ok fine, you can go home but I'm keeping her. So you might as well go get what she needs." He just shook his head at her. He knew it was no use arguing with her.

"Fine Anise." Monte still hadn't talked to Kyah and that was fine with him. He couldn't wait until Anise had his baby. He was hoping for a Jr. "You been staying off your feet?"

"Yes sir but you can still rub them." She wiggled her feet at him and he took them in his hands.

"Anything for you ma." She smiled and continued playing with Aniyah.

"So have you talked to Kyah?" Anise asked. She couldn't understand how a woman gave up their child without a second thought.

"Nah, but it's cool. She can keep her ass wherever the hell she's at."

"Well I'm here for her. I love her like she was mine. I mean how could I not. Look at these cheeks."

"Dadada." Aniyah called out. It was the first time saying it and that made Monte smile.

"Aww she called you. How cute. Now we have to get her to say Anise."

"You funny."

She slapped Monte on the arm. Monte just stared at Anise with his daughter. This was his family and hopefully soon he'd have his son. Then his family would be complete.

Chapter Fourteen

Asha was fixing breakfast when Rahsaan walked in the kitchen. They had been getting alone and actually acting like a married couple. But she knew reality would soon set in and she'd be going back to Atlanta. She hated the fact that she messed up their happy home.

"What's up bae?" he grabbed her from the back placing kisses on her neck.

"Hey. Are the kids woke yet?"

"Bri is but Mell still sleep." He sat down at the table. He knew it was almost time for Asha to go back to Atlanta and he was trying to think of a way to get her to stay. He needed his family.

"Well breakfast is done. I'm going to get the kids." She started out the kitchen but Rahsaan caught her and pulled her down on his lap.

"Rah, what are you doing?" She didn't know why but she was nervous.

"Please don't take my kids away from me again. I need y'all here with me. I know we had our issues but we can work it out ma. I love you. I tried getting over you but I cant."

Asha didn't know what to say. "Rah, I don't know if it's too late. Too much has happened. I would never keep the kids away from you but I live in Atlanta now."

His heart broke in two. Why was she doing this? He didn't cheat on her. It was the other way around.

"I hear you Asha." He pushed her off him and walked away. Asha let a tear drop as she heard the front door close. Was this really it for them? Could she stay and fix this? She was confused but her stubbornness made the decision for her. She was headed back to Atlanta tomorrow.

<><><><>

Asha was combing Brielle's hair. They had an early flight and she wanted to make sure everything was done the night before. Rahsaan was upstairs with Romell watching Rio. He loved spending time with his kids and after tomorrow he didn't know when he'd get to do it again.

"Daddy look." Romell pointed to the TV. "I see man."

A few minutes later Brielle came in and climbed on the bed.

"Daddy you like my hair?"

He pulled her closer and hugged her. "I love it baby girl." The three laid there and watched TV until they fell asleep.

It was 6am and Asha was up getting the kids ready. Rahsaan sat there watching like a lost puppy.

"Mommy I don't want to go. I want my daddy." Brielle whined.

"Bri, we'll be back soon ok." Asha tried to assure her but that didn't stop the crying. Romell was too small to know what was going on. Rahsaan picked up Brielle and walked out the room.

"Look at daddy baby girl." She did. "You know I love you very much right?" She shook her yes.

"I need you to be a big girl for daddy. You have to go with mommy but daddy will be down there to visit you soon ok?"

"Ok." She really wasn't feeling his answer but she was pacified for now.

"Now give me a kiss." He didn't want to let her go. It was the hardest thing he ever had to do but he had to. Asha didn't know if she was doing the right thing but she still decided to leave. Maybe love doesn't conquer all.

<><><><>

Phalon hadn't talked to Lovely in three weeks. She had changed the locks and was ignoring his phone calls. He was ready to murder Melanie. He didn't even know how she got in his office but she hadn't been to work either. He knew when he saw her it was over for her. He wasn't about to tolerate anyone coming in between him and his wife.

He had been staying in a hotel and was beyond ready to go home. He only saw his girls when they were with his mother. He was so stressed that it started to show. He hadn't had a haircut in almost two weeks and he hadn't been to the club. Rahsaan had been taking care of the books and keeping him updated on everything.

Phalon tried calling Lovely to see how she was doing. He knew how hard her pregnancy was with London and wanted to be there for her, even if from a distance. She didn't answer as usual. He knew that if he could just get her to listen to him he could explain to her that he wasn't with Melanie. Then he thought about the surveillance footage at the club. That was his way out of this mess. He could prove that he wasn't even at the club the same time as Melanie. He was happy because he knew eventually he would have his baby back and Melanie was going to pay for this.

Lovely had been sicker than usual. She couldn't hold anything down and she was throwing up blood. She had also been having pains in her stomach for a few days. She finally decided to go to the ER since Phalon's mom had the girls. When she got to the emergency room they took her back immediately because she was pregnant. Numerous test and two hours later Lovely found out she had an ulcer which more than likely was caused by stress. That made her pregnancy high risk and she was put on bed rest for the duration of her pregnancy. She didn't know how she was going to do that when she and Phalon weren't speaking. London required a lot of attention. She prayed that she would bet strong throughout this whole ordeal.

Chapter Fifteen

It had been almost two months since Asha had seen Rahsaan and she missed him like crazy but she just wasn't sure about their relationship. He had been down once since she left to see the kids but he ignored her as if she wasn't there. She did, however, know that she would be seeing him soon. She sat on the edge of the seat and looked at the plus sign on the pregnancy test indicating that she was pregnant. She didn't know what that meant for her and Rahsaan but she knew she was keeping her baby.

Asha decided to call him and tell him. It was only right. She dialed his number and waited for him to answer.

"Hello?" A female answered.

Asha thought she had dialed the wrong number. She looked at the screen and sure enough it was Rahsaan's number. She felt like shit because a few months ago he was trying to get back with her and now he had a female answering his phone.

"Hello?" the female asked again.

Asha just hung up. She decided to send him a message on Fb since his chick was obviously around. She sent the message and then went to lay down. It was after nine so both Brielle and Romell were sleeping. Asha cried herself to sleep. She couldn't believe she let her family fall apart because she cheated.

India was a new girl that Rahsaan had been seeing. She was a pretty girl with mocha colored skin. She rocked her hair in a short pixie cut and she stood 5'4, with small breast but a big ass. She and Rahsaan had been kicking it tough since Asha left a few months ago.

India knew who Asha was. She didn't know the extent of their relationship but she knew she was his ex and the mother of his kids.

"Did my phone ring?" Rahsaan asked when he got out the shower. He thought he heard it but wasn't sure.

"Yeah, it was Asha but she didn't say anything."

He looked at her like she was crazy. "You answered my phone?"

The only person he allowed to invade his space like that was Asha. He liked India but they weren't that deep for her to be answering his phone.

"Well I didn't think it was a problem. I mean you are my man right?" She thought they were a couple even though they had never put a title on what they had.

"Ma, look. I like you but I'm not ready for a relationship. I mean I'm still married. My wife and I are separated but I'm not looking for a relationship."

India was pissed. She knew Rah had money and she wanted a piece of it and she wasn't about to let Asha ruin that for her. She had spent too much time living with her mother and this was her come up.

"Fine Rah. I'm not trying to rush things but I like you a lot and I wanna see where this can go." She put on her best performance but Rah saw right through it. He knew then that it was a wrap between them.

He picked up his phone to dial Asha back but she didn't answer. He saw that he had a Facebook notification and decided to check it and was shocked to say the least. It was from Asha.

Since you got groupie bitches answering your phone now I decided to tell you on here. At least I know you will get the message. I'm pregnant. Congrats you're going to be a daddy again.

"Damn," was all he could say.

Chapter Sixteen

Lovely tried her best to comply with the doctor's orders but it was hard when you're a mom. Now she was suffering the consequences. She was now laying in a hospital bed after delivering a still born baby. She had been having pains in her lower back and she didn't feel the baby moving. That worried her so she went to the ER only to find out her baby had no heartbeat. Normally she would have been released the next day but Lovely was depressed and they were scared to release her. They feared she be a danger to herself so they kept her for a few days to watch over her. She didn't tell anyone what was going on. She just asked Marva, Phalon's mom to keep the girls because she was tired.

She blamed Phalon for losing her baby. She felt that if he wouldn't have cheated, she wouldn't have stressed and got an ulcer that led her to bed rest. She prayed they let her go home tomorrow. All she wanted was to lay in her bed. But laying in that hospital bed she got the sudden desire to call her best friend. She dialed Anise.

Anise answered the phone. "Hey sis. How are you feeling?"

"Not so good."

That alarmed Anise. "What's wrong ma?"

"I lost the baby, " Lovely cried.

"Oh my god. Sis where are you so I can come to you?"

"The hospital. But wait until tomorrow. That way you can drive me home."

"I'm so sorry sis. Wait, where is Pha?"

"I don't know and I don't fucking care! This shit is his fault." Anise felt bad that her girl was going through this. She still hadn't told Lovely she was pregnant and now she really couldn't tell her because she had just lost her baby.

"Well I'll be up there first thing in the morning. Do you need anything?"

"No. but please don't tell Monte because I'm not ready for Phalon to know."

"Ok sis. Get some rest."

Rahsaan had just got off the plane. He was headed to bring Asha and his kids back home. With her being pregnant there was no way he was letting them stay in Atlanta, even if he had to drag her back. He didn't have any luggage because he didn't plan on staying. He got a rental and headed to Asha's house.

It took him about thirty minutes to get to her apartment. He got out and headed to her door. He rang the doorbell and waited for Asha to answer. When she opened the door shock was evident in her face. He didn't mention anything about coming to Atlanta.

"Hey Rah." She stepped aside so that he could come in. Brielle was sitting on the couch watching TV when she saw him.

"Daddy!" She ran to him.

"Hey daddy's baby." He kissed her face.

"You should have told me you were coming, " Asha suggested.

"This isn't a pleasure trip. Now you need to go pack whatever you want to take but y'all are coming home."

"Rah, I am home." The vein in his forehead popped out. He wasn't in the mood to play with Asha.

"Brielle go to your room for a minute." He put his daughter down. "Asha don't play games with me. You know how I roll. Now I'm not asking you, I'm telling you it's time to go home." She rolled her eyes at him. She didn't know who he thought she was but he didn't run shit.

"I'm not leaving Rah." She went to walk away and he grabbed her.

"You think it's a game? The last time you were here pregnant with my baby shit got ugly. That's not about to go down again. Even if you don't want to be with me yo ass is coming home."

She pushed him away. "Wrong."

He collared her up. "Do I have to drag yo ass on the airplane? Because I will have a plane chartered within the hour. I will drag you kicking and screaming if I have to. Now I am trying to give you the opportunity to do this the right way." He spoke through gritted teeth. Asha knew it was a losing battle so she decided to pack what was important and leave with him.

"Fine." Was all she said and he released her.

"Our plane leaves in the morning so you need to be ready and don't fuck with me Asha." He walked to the back of the apartment to find his kids. He couldn't believe she had his kids living in this small ass apartment when they had a big house. She had him fucked up.

Chapter Seventeen

"Are you ok sis?" Anise was sitting with Lovely. She had been home from the hospital for two days and Anise hadn't left her side since. She didn't know what was going on with her and Phalon but she hoped they fixed it soon. It was starting to affect the kids. They knew something was going on between their parents; especially Kimani.

"Yeah I'm good. I just need a nap."

"Well go ahead and take a nap. I got the girls."

When Anise got up to walk out Lovely stopped her. "So when was yo ass gone tell me you were pregnant?"

Anise looked like a deer caught in headlights. "Well the time was never right and I didn't want to add to your stress, especially with you losing the baby."

"Girl shit happens but you're my girl and I'm happy for you, " Lovely said. "Wait, who's the daddy?"

"Monte girl."

"Oh see we gotta talk as soon as I'm feeling better."

"I got you sis." Anise went to go see what the girls were doing. She found them in the family room watching TV.

"Hey divas. What do y'all want for dinner?" She asked as she sat down next to them.

"I don't know," Kimani replied, never taking her eyes off the TV. She wanted her parents to stop fighting and her dad to come home. She hated seeing him only when she went to her nana house.

"Well we can order pizza and watch movies." Anise suggested.

"Ok."

Anise noticed how distant Kimani was. "Kimani is there anything you want to talk about?"

"No, I just want my daddy to come home. I mean I love my mom but I want them here in the same house." Anise smiled at Kimani referring to Lovely as her mom.

"Well sweetie, sometimes adults have disagreements but they will eventually work it out. Your parent's love each other very much and they will get through this ok?"She assured Kimani.

"Ok."

Anise felt bad that kids were put in the middle of adult's mess. She knew she had to have a talk with Lovely and Phalon. They had to fix this shit and fast.

<><><><>

Kimani was in her room when she heard Lovely crying. She didn't know what was wrong but she knew her daddy could fix it so she called him.

"Hey baby girl." Phalon answered.

"Hi daddy. I miss you."

"I miss you too baby. How is your sister and Lovely?"

"London is cool but mommy is not." This was his first time hearing Kimani call Lovely mom and he kind of liked it.

"What do you mean? Is there something wrong with her?"

"I don't know. I mean they think I don't know a lot because I'm a kid but I hear things. And mommy was in the hospital when we were at nana's. Now she's in her room crying and I don't know what is wrong. Please come home daddy and make sure she's ok."

Phalon instantly became alert because Lovely was pregnant and he didn't know what was going on.

"I'm on my way baby girl. I'll call you when I'm outside so you can open the door."

"Ok daddy." Kimani was relieved because she knew her dad could fix it. He was like superman to her.

When Phalon pulled up Kimani had opened the door. She had saw him pull up.

"Hey baby girl." He hugged her.

"Hey daddy."

He headed upstairs to find Lovely. When he walked in the room she was sleep. She looked so peaceful. He just wanted to hold her and tell her everything would be alright. He walked over to her and tapped her. She opened her eyes.

"What the hell are you doing here, " she asked in a calm voice. She didn't have the energy to yell at him.

"Our daughter was worried about you and she called me." He didn't mention the hospital visit because he wanted to see if she would tell him.

"I'm fine. You can leave."

"Cut the bullshit Lovely." She turned away from him. He kicked off his shoes and climbed in bed with her. He tried pulling her to him but she resisted. That didn't stop him.

"Stop running from me. I didn't do shit and if you let me, I can prove it."

She just laid there.

"Baby look at me please."

She didn't move.

"Lovely." She still didn't move. He turned her around to face him. "I love you ma. I would never hurt you intentionally. I didn't do anything with that girl. I wasn't even in the club at the same time with her and I have proof. I just want to be here for you and my kids." He rubbed her belly and that's when he realized it was flat. He panicked because she should have been showing being almost seven months.

"Lovely please tell me you didn't kill my seed."

"No. I lost him."

His heart broke. He should have been here for her. He blamed himself for their lost.

"Baby I'm sorry." He just held her as she cried. He promised from that moment on that he die protecting his family. He vowed to never be the cause of her tears again.

Chapter Eighteen

Asha had been back in Detroit for three days. She hadn't seen Rah since he dropped them off at the house. Pissed was an understatement. She couldn't believe he had the nerve to come get her and then disappear. She was ready to tell him to kiss her ass but she didn't know what his crazy ass would do.

What she didn't understand was why he sweating her if he had a bitch. She shook her head.

"Mommy where's daddy?" Brielle walked in the room bringing Asha back to her thoughts.

"I'll call him baby." She picked up her cell phone and dialed Rah's number.

He actually answered. "What's up ma?" she heard music in the background.

"Bri wants to talk to you." She passed Brielle the phone.

"Daddy are you coming home?" Bri didn't understand that her parents weren't together or that her dad didn't live there.

"I'll be there soon baby, ok?" He was with India but he'd drop anything for his kids. And if his daughter needed him then he'd be there.

"Ok daddy." She passed Asha the phone. She hung up. She didn't have shit to say to him.

"Ok go on upstairs and put on your pajamas. I'll be up there in a few."

"Ok mommy." Brielle ran up the stairs and Asha picked a sleeping Romell up off the couch and carried him upstairs. Times like this she needed Rah around. He was getting bigger and heavier but it was what it was.

Rah walked in the house a hour later. He would have been there sooner but India was giving him a hard time. He knew it was time to let her go. She was becoming a problem plus Tracy wouldn't stop calling him. She even popped up at his apartment last week.

Asha was sitting on the couch watching TV when he walked in.She didn't even acknowledge his presence.

"Well, hello to you too."

She gave him the finger.

"I love you too." He headed upstairs to Brielle's room.

She was still woke watching Disney channel. "What are you doing up little girl?" He sat down on her bed.

"I was waiting for you daddy." She climbed in his lap and he just held her. He loved being a father.

"Well I'm her lil' lady and I'll be here when you wake up. Now get some sleep." He laid her down and pulled the covers over her. He went to check on Romell and he was in his bed sleep. Perfect time to chill with Asha. He wanted to make things right with her and he knew it was going to take some time but he wasn't going to stop until he had his wife back.

Asha was in the same spot when Rah came back downstairs. He sat down next to her.

"What are you watching?"

"The best man holiday." She said, never taking her eyes off of the TV.

"So we having another baby huh?" He pulled her to him and rubbed her stomach.

"Yeah." She pushed his hands off of her.

"I can't touch you?"

"Not when you was just laid up with another bitch."

He smiled. "I wasn't laid up. I was out kicking it."

"Whatever Rah."

He pulled her back in his arms and kissed her neck. "Do you love me Asha?"

"Of course. You're my first love, my kid's father and my husband. Even if we aren't together, I'll always love you Rah."

"I love you too ma." He held her as they watched TV. A good hour went by when his phone rang.

"Hello?"

It was India and she was mad because he told her he'd come see her after he saw about his daughter but he never went nor did he call her.

"Man chill out with that yelling shit, " Rah barked back.

Asha sat up and took the phone from him and he let her.

"Look, India he will catch you later. It's family time right now." She hung up and turned his phone off.

Rah smiled because slowly his wife was returning. They cuddled and watched TV until they fell asleep.

Chapter Nineteen

India was beyond pissed. Rahsaan was supposed to be hers but his bitch ass wife came and ruined shit. He cussed her out for answering his phone but it was alright for Asha to get on and disrespect her. She had revenge on her mind and it wasn't nice.

India had someone that hated Asha just as much as she did. Asha would pay for ruining her life.

Anise was approaching her fifth month of pregnancy and the sickness had subsided. Monte was taking good care of her and although they hadn't made it official that was her boo thang. She had been helping him take care of Aniyah full time because her mother still wanted nothing to do with her. She was just trife but Anise didn't mind. She had come to love Monte's daughter as her own.

Today she was taking Aniyah to Lovely's house for a play date with London and Brielle. Plus she would be able to catch up with her girls. She dressed Aniyah and combed her hair which was long for a one year old.

"Ok mama let's go have fun." She picked Aniyah up and they headed out the door. She was strapping her in the car seat when Monte pulled up.

"Where y'all headed too ma," he asked as he kissed her lips.

"To Lovely's. Aniyah has a playdate with London and Brielle."

"Oh, ok. Well I'm tired as hell so I'm going to take a nap but I'm staying here with you tonight." They still had their separate houses but it was rare that they went to sleep without each other.

"Be careful bae." He went in the house and she got in the car and drove off.

When she pulled up to Lovely's house Asha was already there. She was ready to unwind and kick it. She grabbed Aniyah's bag and got her out the car seat. They walked hand in hand up the walkway ready to enjoy their day.

Kyah was pissed at Monte for having her daughter around Anise. She didn't understand what he saw in her. She knew having Aniyah would seal the deal for them That was why she drugged him. He thought he cheated on Anise willingly and had been carrying the guilt around all this time when really he was drugged. She wanted him the first time she saw him but Anise got to him first. They had met at the annual hood basketball tournament and he never called her. A few weeks later she found out why............... Anise.

She vowed to make Anise pay. She wanted Monte and if she couldn't have him then Anise wouldn't either. Hell, for all she cared, Aniyah could go too. She wasn't trying to play mama. All she wanted was Monte and since he didn't want her, she didn't want the baby.

She picked up the phone and called the one person that understood her. The one person that could help her get Anise back. Yes revenge was sweet and she could practically taste it.

"Hey can you meet me? I'm ready to put that plan in motion." Kyah spoke into the phone.

"Name the place."

"I'll text you in a few, don't be late." She hung up with a smile on her face.

Chapter Twenty

King and Ryan were having a cook out at their house. Ryan wanted to get all of their close friends and family there. Family was important to her and she didn't want any of them losing sight of that. Everyone was there. Helen, who was King's mom, Mia and Harlem, Kita and Markie, Yvette and Tez, Javon and Trina, Asha and Rahsaan, Lovely and Phalon, Anise and Monte and all of their children. She even invited Marva, Phalon's mom, and Darlene, Rahsaan's mom, and Mama Rose, Harlem's mom.

Everything was perfect. They had food and drinks. The kids were playing and everyone was having a good time. The only person missing was Stone and he said he would be there. Ryan looked at Rahsaan and Asha and smiled. Yeah they claimed not to be together but a blind man could see that they were in love.

She walked over to where King was and sat on his lap. He was her heart, her other half. She was his Bonnie. They had been through so much together and still came out on top.

"What's up bae?" He kissed her lips.

"Nothing, just seeing what yall up too."

"Aint shit. Just kicking it." Mia was sitting next to Harlem admiring the love King and Ryan shared. She was so happy for them.

"Well come on Ry, let's go see what these kids are up to." Mia suggested but before she could get up Stone walked in the backyard with Kyah. Of course she got ghetto. She walked over to Monte.

"Why the fuck do ya bitch got my baby Monte? Huh?"

If looks could kill she'd be dead. "First off, get the fuck out of my face. Second, Aniyah aint seen yo ass in almost two months so miss me with that bullshit." He walked over to Anise who was holding Aniyah.

"You good ma?" He knew Anise temper and he didn't need her acting a fool with his baby in her belly.

"I'm good. Aint no bitch this way. What I wanna know is why Stone with ya baby mama?" Monte wanted to know that too. Too bad Lovely beat him to it.

"What the fuck is this Stone? You rocking with this thot now?"She was pissed at her brother for messing with her and bringing her here.

"I am. What's the problem? I mean he didn't want her. He threw her to the side for community pussy." He laughed as he pointed to Anise.

That was all it took for Monte. His fist connected with Stones face and they were going at it. Stone was so high that he was no match for Monte.

"Stop it! Stop right now! Pha do something, " Lovely yelled.

Phalon pulled Monte off Stone even though he wanted to let him keep going. That was his wife's brother though and he couldn't let them fight.

"You two need to leave." Mia spoke up. She didn't know Stone but she could tell he was trouble. Stone looked around at everybody with blood dripping from his mouth.

"Fuck all y'all." He walked off with Kyah trailing behind. Once again she left her baby.

"Alright shows over. Let's party!" Mia yelled. And that's exactly what they did.

Asha was standing at the food table making a plate when Rah walked over and grabbed her by the waist.

"I love you Asha." He kissed her neck.

"I love you too Rah." She really did. She was just scared to get back with him out of fear of him leaving her because of what she did. On top of that Zierre had started back calling her. She ignored his calls but he wouldn't stop calling her.

"As long as you know."

She rolled her eyes. Yeah she knew he loved her but he was still laying up with his bitch and Asha was cool with being by herself. She had kids to think about anyway.

"Can I come home with you tonigh, " he asked.

"What's wrong? Ya girl aint giving you none?"

"You got jokes."

"Who joking? You aint been laid up with me since I came back. I mean you came to the house and stayed one night and that was only because Brielle wanted you too. So don't come at me with that bullshit now. Yeah I know I fucked up and I'm paying for it every day but don't keep toying with my feelings Rah." She walked away Leaving him standing there.

He knew she was right. He was still messing with India but he wanted his wife back. He needed to dead that before he lost his wife for good.

Chapter Twenty- One

"So you're breaking up with me because your wife is back, " India asked Rah.

"Man India, I have fun with you but we both knew what it was. I love my wife. We were going through some shit but I'm ready to work it out with her."

"Well make sure you have time for your child."

He looked confused. "What the hell are you talking about India?"

"That's right. I'm pregnant. So make sure you tell ya wife that she has a step child on the way. Now you can see yourself out." She turned and walked away. She was hurt because in the process of chasing a dollar she fell in love with Rah. But reality was he'd never be hers.

Rah walked out of the apartment, trying to figure out his next move. Asha was going to kill him. What he couldn't understand was how India ended up pregnant. He strapped up with her every time. Something told him he'd lose his family for sure now.

Stone couldn't believe Anise was playing house with Monte. He had worked too hard to show her he was the one for her but she was so into Monte that she couldn't see it. He was out for blood. He hated Monte because he had the woman he wanted and needed. Monte had to pay and Stone was ready to make it happen. If his plan went well Anise would be his.

"Come suck my dick." Monte told Kyah as he snorted the lines of coke that were spread out on the coffee table. He was higher than a kite and horny. It was like déjà vu all over again. Kyah didn't do it for him but she'd do until Anise came to her senses.

Kyah hated Stone. She originally solicited him to help her get Anise away from Monte but he started beating her ass and making her do shit she didn't want to do. He even got her hooked on coke. This made her hate Anise even more because she felt she was the reason Monte and now Stone treated her like shit. She didn't know what it was about Anise that had them gone but she wanted her ass dead.

The bitch even got my baby. She thought. Kyah got down on her knees in front of Stone and pulled his dick out. He was fine but his attitude made him disgusting. If the circumstances was different and he wasn't on drugs, she would have gotten with him. But that wasn't the case. He was supposed to be helping her get Monte back but it seemed as if he was the one on the receiving end. She knew something had to give soon because she didn't know how much more of Stone she could take.

Kyah gagged as he pushed his dick down her throat. She almost threw up but held it down. She didn't need a repeat of the last time. Stone had beat her ass for throwing up on him while giving head. Kyah was just ready for this nightmare to be over.

Stone was in his own world. He was plotting his revenge against Anise and Monte. Yeah Monte had her first but she still belonged to him and he would stop at nothing to have her. He felt if he couldn't have her than no one would. Even if he had to kill her.

Tracy had been watching Asha for almost two weeks. She needed to know what it was about her that kept Rahsaan going back. Tracy felt played because she was always there for him but she always got his ass to kiss when Asha showed up. She had to admit though, Asha was a pretty girl with a nice shape but hell so was she. One thing was for sure, she wasn't ready to give Rah up this time. She was prepared to fight for her man, wife or not.

Chapter Twenty-Two

"Let's go away ma, " Phalon told Lovely as they lay in bed. He had been stressed and he knew she was. She had lost their son and it took a toll on both of them. Things were ok between them but still strained. Even though Phalon was able to prove he wasn't cheating, that feeling was still lingering in the back of Lovely's head. For that reason alone she couldn't be with her husband like she wanted to. When they had sex it was forced and that was if he was at home.

He didn't know what to do to show Lovely that it was all about her. He cherished the ground she walked on but she was too stubborn to open her eyes and see it.

"I can't leave London, " was her response.

Phalon felt it was a bunch of bullshit because his mother would gladly take London. But he wasn't going to press the issue.

"Fine." He got up out the bed and walked out the room.

Lovely wanted to trust her husband but it was hard. He may have proved his innocence in that situation but that didn't make up for the unexplained late nights and her woman's intuition. It didn't help that she was dealing with the death of her baby. It was as if she was mourning by herself. Phalon never wanted to talk about it. It was like it never happened and that pissed her off.

Phalon didn't know what was happening between him and his wife but he didn't like it. It was like she had flipped the script overnight. She definitely wasn't the woman he fell in love with. Something had to change soon or he didn't know if he could stay.

Rahsaan had been staying at the house with Asha and the kids. He hadn't talked to India in over two weeks. She was surprisingly quiet. He had a fear that Asha would find out India was pregnant..........If she really was. He hoped like hell that this was a game. He knew if India was pregnant by him that he and Asha would be over for sure.

"Daddy can we go to the park?" Brielle asked. Rahsaan looked at his daughter. She looked so much like him and was getting bigger. He loved his family and he was ready to do what he had to in order to keep them.

"Let's see what mommy is doing first." He picked Brielle up and they headed upstairs. Asha was sleep.

"Well mommy is asleep so let's get your brother and go to the park." Rahsaan took the kids to the park and let Asha rest. He couldn't wait to see what they were having. He was hoping she gave him another girl.

They had been at the park for a few hours and Rahsaan was ready to go but Brielle and Romell weren't. He knew what would make them ready.

"Let's go and get ice cream guys." They screamed and ran towards him. He took their hand and walked them to the car.

"Get in your seat and buckle up Bri." He said as he buckled Romell. He got in and they headed to Dairy Queen.

Rahsaan loved spending time with his kids. He could remember a time when he envied King and Harlem for having what he wanted. They had the kids and the wife and now he had the kids but not the wife. He felt his wife slipping away slowly and he didn't know if they would ever be the same. He found himself praying on a regular. Something his mom always taught him to do. He was a hustler but that didn't mean he didn't believe in a higher power.

"Daddy this is good, " Brielle said in between spoons of her ice cream

"I'm glad you're enjoying it baby. We gotta take mommy some home." Brielle agreed as she ate her ice cream. He lived for moments like this and he was even happier that Asha was giving him another baby. He wasn't the type to have kids by a bunch of women. He wanted them all to have the same mama but that wish seemed short lived, especially if India was telling the truth about carrying his baby.

Rahsaan had his hopes up high. He knew things with Asha wouldn't be the same overnight but he was willing to try. The only problem was Asha's stubbornness. She knew she was the one that fucked up but she also knew he was messing with India and that was something she wasn't cool with.

<><><><>

Rahsaan hadn't spoken to India since he broke things off with her two weeks ago but she was still texting and calling him. Unbeknownst to him, Asha had answered one of those calls. Asha was far from naïve but she had let India get to her head.

.... *"Hello?" Asha answered groggily. Normally she didn't answer his phone being that they weren't together but he was dead sleep and it wouldn't stop ringing.*

"Yeah is Rah there?" It was India; Asha would never forget her voice.

"He's sleep." She responded in a sarcastic tone.

"Well tell him his girl called."

"Who is this?" Asha played dumb.

"Let's not play games Asha. You know exactly who this is. Just tell our man to call me." India hung up. Asha was beyond tired of India...............

"Mommy can I have some juice?" Brielle asked bringing her back to the present..

"Come on baby." Asha stood and followed Brielle to the kitchen. Romell was hanging with Rahsaan today so it was just her and Brielle. She wasn't complaining either because Romell was a handful. Asha poured Brielle's juice and sat her down at the table. Realizing what time it was she decided to start dinner. Even though Rah was with India, or so she thought, Asha still cooked, cleaned and took care of home. That was her husband, plus she felt responsible for their problems.

"Mommy where's my daddy?" Brielle was a true daddy's girl.

"He and Mell are hanging out. They'll be home soon." Asha told her as she prepared the chicken that she was about to cook.

"Ok. I'm going to watch TV." Brielle ran off and Asha smiled at how big she was. She was three going on thirty.

<><><><>

Asha was almost done with dinner when she heard Rah come in. He didn't come in the kitchen until ten minutes later and she didn't hear Romell running around which only meant one thing. He was sleep. When Rah walked in the kitchen he smiled at his wife. He loved the fact that she still took care of home despite their problems. He walked over and grabbed her from behind.

"What's up wife?" he kissed her neck.

As much as Asha loved the affection she pushed him off of her. "Move Rah!"

He didn't move. "What's ya problem ma?"

She pushed him again. Rahsaan was confused. He reached in front of her and turned off the stove before turning her to face him.

"I'm trying to kick it with my wife so tell me what the fuck your problem is." He was pissed and horny.

"India is the fucking problem! You're not about to lay up with yo bitch and then come home and fuck me!" She yelled a little louder than she meant to.

"First off, I'll never fuck you. You're the only female I make love to. Second, I'm not fucking with nobody else. I'm too busy trying to get back right with you. Yeah we got our issues but I wanna work it out. I love you Asha. That shit with India is dead. You aint got shit to worry about because I would never disrespect you like that."

Asha was speechless.

For what seemed like forever they just stared at each other.

"Ma, I love you with everything in me, " Rah said breaking the silence. "You hurt a nigga and I tried to get over you but I can't because you're here." He said pointing to his heart.

Asha let the tears fall that she had been holding back. Rah took her in his arms and kissed her tears away.

"Don't cry baby. I'm here and I aint going nowhere." He held her close. He had never loved another woman. He had been in love with Asha since they were young teens. She was his first teenage love affair. The one he gave his last name too and no one could ever come between that. Their bond was too strong.

"Look at me ma." He lifted her chin so that she was looking in his eyes. "Do you love me, " he asked looking in her eyes.

Asha just shook her head yes. Rah kissed her pouty lips. He kissed her with so much passion that she felt her knees go weak. Rah let his hands roam all over her body. He missed the way she felt in his arms. He kissed her neck while his hands fondled her breast. Asha let out a soft moan. He kissed her lips again and this time he parted her lips and she sucked his tongue. Rah pulled the drawstring on her jogging pants and pushed them down. Pushing her thong to the side he inserted one and then two fingers. She was soaking wet and he was ready to feast on her kitty.

"Wait Rah! Brielle…" He hushed her with another kiss. He had already checked on Brielle when he laid Romell down.

"She's sleep, now shut up." Asha complied. He ripped her thong off and picked her up. He walked her over to the counter and sat her on it. Bending down he went in head first. He loved how she always tasted sweet because of the fruit she ate.

"Ooh shit Rah!" she leaned her head back an arched her back. She hadn't had any type of sexual encounter in a while. She was in heaven. He stuck his finger inside her while he ate her pussy. That took over the edge. Her legs shook and she came. Rah licked up every drop before getting up.

The look of pure satisfaction was on her face. That made him want more.

"Come on let's go upstairs." He helped her down and led the way upstairs. Rah stripped out of his clothes and took her shirt off.

"Lay down baby." She did and he climbed between her thick thighs. He licked and sucked on her breast which always got her going. That was her spot.

"Fuck! Put it in Rah." She begged. She needed and wanted the dick. Her body craved him. She knew he was about to put it down because he was a beast in bed. He rubbed the head up and down on her clit, teasing her.

"You ready for daddy?" He asked.

"Yes."

That was all he need to hear.

Chapter Twenty-Three

Lovely and Phalon's marriage was still on the rocks. Both were stubborn and blamed the other for the loss of their baby. Phalon more so because he really wanted a son. All he and Lovely did was fight. Most of the time over stupid stuff. Phalon would start a fight just so he'd have an excuse to leave the house.

The constant bickering caused Phalon to stay out sometimes all night. Needless to say Lovely was fed up. She didn't understand how they ended up like this. They were like strangers living together. They didn't talk anymore and the sex was non-existent. When he did stay at the house he slept on the couch. Lovely, being a woman, just knew he had another chick on the side. Aint no way he was going without sex. She remember expressing her concerns with her girls one night. They were chilling at Ryan's house when she felt the need to vent.

"I think Pha is cheating." She blurted out after drinking her third glass of wine.

"Come on now. That nigga worships the ground you walk on," Anise replied. She just couldn't believe that Phalon would cheat on Lovely.

"Well he fucking somebody because he damn sure aint fucking me. It's been damn near two months since we've been intimate. On top of that his ass been staying out late, sometimes all night. So you tell me what the fuck he doing?" Ryan was speechless and Asha just shook her head.

"Damn sis. I'm sorry." Was Anise's response.

"Fuck that Lovely! Don't go jumping to conclusions with no proof. Talk to him and find out the deal." Ryan replied. She hated to see her girl go through this. She had grown to love Lovely like a sister.

"I'm not jumping to conclusions but I'm far from dumb. I'm good on his ass." Lovely's mind was made up. She was leaving.

"Well whatever you decide, just know we're here for you." Ryan hugged her. She really hoped that they worked out their issues.

Stone had been on one. Yeah he was down with RBM but he wasn't getting the type of money they was. He felt like a bitch working for his sister's husband. He knew Phalon only put him on because of Lovey and he wasn't feeling that.

Stone had larceny in his heart. He felt he should have been sitting in Rahsaan's position. Had he not got locked up, he'd be running Detroit. He was ready to put his plan in motion but what he failed to realize was, RBM's reach was far too long. Going up against them was like going to a gun fight without a gun.

Stone sat in his car watching Phalon. He had to take out the head first and being that Rahsaan was dealing with his marriage issues that left Phalon in charge. He had been plotting against RBM for some time now. His *I don't care* attitude accompanied with the drug habit he had developed clouded his better judgment. It didn't bother him that killing Phalon would hurt his sister and niece. Greed was an ugly monster and sometimes got the best of people.

<><><><>

Lovely had packed her things and was headed out the door. She looked around the house she shared with her husband and cried. It was really over. She had London in her arms and Kimani was with her nana so this was easier for her. She wasn't ready to explain to Mani why she was leaving.

She wiped her face and headed out the door. She didn't bother calling Phalon to tell him she was leaving. What was the use? He'd know when he brought his ass home eventually. Lovely had found a three bedroom condo in Southfield. Phalon spent so much time away from home that he never knew his wife was planning to leave him. But he was learn today.

When Phalon walked in he expected to see London running about but it was quiet. He didn't park in the garage or he would have known Lovely was gone. He actually felt bad that they had been going through their issues. He loved his wife and knew it was time to stop being stubborn. He headed upstairs to take a shower. When he went to the closet to get his clothes he noticed Lovely's side was empty. He looked in the drawers.......... same thing. He walked to London's room and saw that most of her clothes were gone too. His heartbeat quickened. His wife had left him.

"Fuck!" he punched a hole in the wall. He couldn't believe she was gone. He called her phone only for it to go to voicemail. He tossed the phone at the wall causing it shatter into pieces. He was lost without Lovely and didn't know where to start in getting her back. He just hoped that it wasn't too late.

Lovely had been in her condo for a week and hadn't spoken to Phalon once. She was picking Kimani up today to spend the weekend with her. She was still at Phalon's mother house.

"Come on London so we can go get your sister."

"Yay."

Lovely smiled at her active baby who would be turning three soon. Lovely headed out the door holding London's hand. She helped London in her seat and buckled her before getting in and pulling off.

When Lovely pulled up there was a cocaine white Jag in the driveway.

"Come on baby, " she said as she opened the door for London. London took off running.

"Slow down befo" Her words were caught in her throat. Phalon walked out the door and scooped London up.

"Daddy!"

He kissed her chubby cheeks.

"Hey baby girl. Daddy missed you."

She hugged his neck.

"Go in and get your sister." He put her down and she headed inside.

"So what's up Lovely?" He casually asked even though he wanted to choke the shit out of her ass.

"Hey, " she offered. "I just came by to pick up Kimani."

"Yeah aight. Well drop my kids off to me this weekend." He walked towards his car and got in. he rolled down his window.

"Ayo ma, you foul ass fuck!" He pulled off.

Lovely walked inside the house. She wasn't going there with him.

Chapter Twenty-Four

Things between Anise and Monte had been going good. Even though they never officially got back together, it was sort of unspoken. Monte was happy that Anise was carrying his baby. He catered to her and made sure she had everything she needed or wanted. He rubbed her feet and back. He was even spending less time in the streets.

Today was a chill day for Monte and all he wanted was to be up under Anise and his daughter. Aniyah had become a big part of Anise life. Especially since Kyah wanted nothing to do with her. Monte loved the way Anise took care of his daughter and knew that she'd be a good mom to their unborn. He hadn't heard from Kyah in a few weeks. And he wasn't bothered by it at all.

When he walked in the house Anise and Aniyah were on the couch sleep. He didn't bother them. Instead, he headed to the room and laid down. He had been in the streets all week and was dead tired.

It was Ryan's birthday and King was throwing her a party at Epiphany. He went all out from open bar to all you can eat. It was an all-white event. King made sure she had nothing but the best, she was his queen.

"Yo make sure her gift is there on time man, " King told Rah. He didn't want nothing going wrong. He couldn't wait to see Ryan's face when he gave her his gift.

"I got you man. Just go and get ready. I'll see you in a few hours." Rah gave King dap and headed out. He had to get dressed and go pick up Ryan's gift.

When he got home Asha was already dressed and had his clothes out.

"Thank you baby." He kissed her lips before heading to the shower.

<><><><>

Phalon and Lovely still weren't talking unless it was concerning the kids. Even though he acted as if he didn't care, it was fucking with him not to be with his wife. Tonight though, all he wanted to do was party and say fuck all his problems.

He checked his outfit one last time before heading out the door. He had to pick up his date. Yup, since Lovely didn't want him he was moving on. He wasn't in the business of chasing nobody. He was doing him.

Chapter Twenty-Five

Lovely walked in the Epiphany looking like a million bucks. One couldn't deny that she was a bad bitch and all eyes were on her. She wore a white sheer Gucci dress that stopped mid-thigh. The only parts of her body you couldn't see were her private areas. She had on silver Gucci pumps that made her long legs look amazing. Her hair was bone straight and had a part down the middle.

"Damn bitch if I wasn't with Rah and I liked pussy I'd take you home tonight." Asha commented when Lovely walked into the VIP section.

"Thanks!" Lovely laughed.

"That dress is bad ass, " Asha complimented.

"Thanks boo. So where is Ryan's ass?" Lovely looked around for her girl.

"They haven't got here yet but Mia and them just walked in." Asha pointed towards the door. Everybody had come out to celebrate Ryan's day.

"Damn it's live as hell in here." Lovely bopped her head to the music. Monte and Rah were kicking it with a few RBM members while the women chilled.

"So how is the pregnancy treating you ladies?" Lovely asked Anise and Asha.

"Girl, I'm tired of this shit already." Asha joked.

"I'm having a good pregnancy plus Monte makes it easier for me.

"Aww, I'm so happy for y'all."

"Hey Ladies." Mia, Kita, and Yvette greeted as they walked up. Before they could respond the DJ announced Ryan and King's arrival.

"Put ya muthafuckin hands together for my boy King and his First Lady Ryan. They doing it big tonight y'all. Hood royalty at its finest." Ryan walked in, hand in hand with King and they made their way to VIP.

Ryan greeted her people.

"Hey boo. Happy birthday." Mia hugged Ryan followed by the rest of the crew.

"Thank yall for coming to celebrate with me. But where the hell is Pha?" Ryan was happy to have everyone here with her but she didn't see him anywhere. She knew he and Lovely were separated but he was still family.

"Oh shit!" Monte said without thinking. Anise turned towards the door to see what he was looking at. Phalon had just walked in with a chick on his arm. A bad one too.

"No this muthafucka didn't." Anise stood up fuming. She couldn't believe how Phalon was playing her girl.

"Sit yo ass down with my seed in yo belly, " Monte said. He thought Phalon was wrong but that was between him and Lovely. He knew how Anise was about her friend but he wasn't gone have her stressing out while she was carrying his baby.

Lovely was pissed but you would never be able to tell by her facial expression. Yeah they were separated but that shit he just pulled was mad disrespectful.

"Bae go talk to ya boy because I'm not about to have no drama at my party, " Ryan said, whispering in King's ear as Phalon and his date approached the VIP section.

"I got it ma." King stood up and walked over to Phalon.

"Aye man let me holla at you for a sec." They walked away leaving Phalon's date alone.

"Man are you trying to die tonight, " King asked Phalon.

"Nah but she aint fucking with me so why do I have to stay single? That was her choice man."

"I hear you man. Just keep control of the situation because you see Lovely got all her girls here and you know how they get down." King warned.

"I hear you man." Phalon walked back to his date and King to his wife.

"Hey Ry, happy birthday ma." Phalon leaned down and kissed her cheek before passing her a gift box."

"Thanks brother." She replied as she mugged his date.

"Whose ya friend, " she asked him.

"Oh, this is Toya. Toya this is the birthday girl Ryan and the rest of the crew." He didn't acknowledge Lovely at all.

"Hi Toya, I'm Anise and this is my best friend and Phalon's wife Lovely."

Phalon bit the inside of his jaw to keep from saying anything to Anise. She needed to know her place and being in his and Lovely's business wasn't it.

"I don't have time for this reality TV shit. I'm out." Lovely got up and walked away.

"You know you wrong as hell Phalon." Mia rolled her eyes at him as she and Ryan followed Lovely.

"Man if I don't get no pussy because my wife wanna talk about how wrong you are I'm fucking you up," Harlem replied. Everyone laughed but Harlem knew all too well what was gone happen. These young dudes had a lot to learn when it came to their wives.

"Hey sis are you ok?" Ryan asked Lovely.

"I'm good. I just can't believe he would disrespect me like that. I thought I knew him but I guess his true colors are showing. I'm sorry to ruin your night Ry but I gotta get the hell out of here before I fuck him up." Lovely hugged Ryan and Mia.

"Well call us and let us know you made it home ok?" Mia told her as she got in her car.

"I will. Go back in and enjoy y'all selves."

Chapter Twenty-Six

India was five months pregnant and hadn't spoken to Rahsaan since he walked out her apartment. That was four months ago. She never thought she'd be pregnant and alone but she was. It was time to pay his wife a visit and let her know the deal.

When India pulled up to the house that Rahsaan shared with his wife jealousy and envy was all over her face. She couldn't believe they were living like this and she was living in a one bedroom apartment. Although her one bedroom was a far cry from living with her mother it still wasn't shit. India got out of the car and waddled up to the door. She rang the bell and waited for someone to answer.

When Asha opened the door India was shocked. She recognized her from the pictures Rah had of her in his phone. She never expected Asha to be pregnant too.

"Yes can I help you?" Asha asked when she opened the door.

"Actually you can. I'm India."

Asha was pissed that Rah's side hoe had the nerve to be on her doorstep. "Again what can I do for you?" This time she asked with sarcasm.

"Well, since your husband is dodging my calls, can you tell him we're having a girl and my due date is March 1st."

"Look sweetie, I don't know what you thought you'd gain by coming to my house but make this the last time it happens. As far as your baby, call me when it's born and then and only then will my husband make an appearance to take a DNA test." With that Asha slammed the door in her face.

India was pissed. She didn't get the reaction from Asha that she wanted. She just hoped that when her daughter was born Rahsaan would be around.

Asha was pissed that India was pregnant and claiming her husband to be the father. One thing for sure was Rah had some explaining to do.

<><><><>

Lovely and Phalon had been co-parenting and so far it was going well. Both the girls were living with Lovely full time but Phalon got them on the weekends. Today Lovely was kid free because Marva had the girls. Anise was almost due so Monte had her on house arrest and Asha was just as pregnant. She called Ryan to see if she wanted to hang out. She needed to get out of the house.

"Hey sis, what you doing, " Lovely asked when Ryan answered the phone.

"Chilling with the hubby. What's up mama?"

"Oh nothing. I was kid free and bored as hell."

"Well, I'm in the house for the night but go out girl and have a drink or two. Go let ya hair down." Lovely laughed.

"Girl, enjoy your time with the hubs. I'll hit you up later." She hung up and decided to head to Snookers and have a drink."

When Lovely walked into the pool hall it wasn't too crowded. She found a seat at the bar and ordered a Long Island. She scanned the place as she waited for her drink. It felt weird being out without her husband or her girls.

"Excuse me Ms. Lady, can I sit here and talk to you for a minute?"

Lovely turned around to see who the deep baritone voice belonged to. She was pleased. He was a fine chocolate brotha with a deep dimple in his chin. He looked as if he was about 5'11 and muscular.

"Sure." *Why not* she thought. She was single. She never saw Phalon sitting in the back corner watching her every move. He had saw her from the time she walked in the door. He was there with Toya but he couldn't deny how good his wife looked.

"So what's your name?" Mr. Fine asked Lovely.

"Lovely, and yours?"

"Damon." He smiled showing his perfectly white teeth.

"Nice to meet you Damon."

Phalon was pissed. He didn't like the way dude was making his wife smile. At that moment he knew he had to do what he needed to get her back. He was the only one that was supposed to make her smile.

Lovely had no intentions on talking to Damon outside of the pool hall but it felt good to have attention from a man. She was still in love with her husband and hoped that one day they would get things back to the way they used to be.

Lovely was so caught up in her conversation with Damon that she let the time slip away. It was well after midnight and she knew it was time to head home.

"Well, it's been ice talking to you Damon but I have to be going."

"Well can I get a number so we can get together for dinner?" he asked.

"Probably not. I'm going through a separation and I'm not ready to date."

He shook his head in understanding. "Ok cool. Well at least let me walk you to your car. It's late and I would hate for something to happen to you."

She smiled and accepted his offer. Not that she was scared because she had her .22 in her purse and as they exited the building she put her hand on it. Damon walked her to the car and they said their goodbyes before she got in the car and left.

When Lovely got home she showered and decided to watch Netflix. She was still bored out of her mind. There was no little feet running around the house or no preteen walking around with the phone glued to her ear.

There was no husband to cook for and wait up on. Lovely let the tears fall that had been trying to seep past her eyelids. She realized just how much she missed her family. She missed being a wife and full time mom. She decided to text Phalon to see what he was doing. She missed him like crazy.

Me: Hey, WYD?

Hubby: Chilling. What's up?

Phalon had left the pool hall after seeing Lovely kicking it with dude for a good hour. That was all he could stand. It took everything in him not to snatch her up. He just left and took Toya home.

Me: Nothing, just checking on you.

Phalon smiled. He liked the fact that she still cared even if she pretended not too.

Hubby: So you do love me?

Lovely smiled.

Me: Of course bae

Phalon: Bae huh?

Me: Boy please. I always call you that.

Hubby: yeah ok. Well get some rest sexy. Love you

Me: Love you too.

Lovely was feeling like a teenager with a crush. She was hopefull that they would get their shit together.

Chapter Twenty-Seven

Phaon was ready to get his wife back. He knew that he had to come correct if he wanted things back to normal. He had to date her again. Show her why she fell in love with him in the first place. It was a challenge because Lovely was stubborn but he was up for the challenge.

He ordered her twenty boxes of long stem roses in different colors and three edible arrangements. He had them all sent to her this morning. He signed the card as a secret admirer. He didn't want her to know it was him just yet. He asked his mom to keep the girls for the weekend so he could take Lovely out of town. He was chartering a private plane to Vegas. She didn't know but he asked Ryan to get her there. But first she had a few steps to follow.

"Ok Ry about 5:30 or so I want you to give her the first gift, " Phalon said into the phone.

"Got you. This is so cute what you're doing for her." Ryan was glad to see Phalon doing what he had to for his family.

"Thanks. I love that girl man. It took us separating for me to realize that I was losing a good thing."

"Well don't mess up this time."

"I won't. Thanks for helping me Ryan."

"No thanks needed."

They hung up and Phalon headed to the shower to get ready.

<><><><>

Ryan had talked Lovely into going to the salon with her to get their hair done. Lovely didn't have anything to do so she went along not knowing it was a reason behind it.

"Ok I'm out of here sis but, before I go, this is from your hubby." Ryan passed Lovely the envelope. She was confused but opened it.

From the moment I laid eyes on you I knew you'd be mine. I love you.

Lovely smiled. She didn't know what kind of game Phalon was playing but she was going to play along.

"Well come on let's go." Ryan drove Lovely to the house she used to share with Phalon.

"What are we doing here?" Lovely asked confused.

"Just get ya ass out and come on."

When they walked in the house there was a make-up artist and stylist there.

"Hello, Mrs. Mitchell. We are your glam squad courtesy of your husband."

Lovely smiled. She didn't know what Phalon was up to but she went along with it.

Once Lovely's make-up was done and the stylist had dressed her, she looked amazing.

"Damn sis, you look hot, " Ryan complimented her. Well come on so I can get you to your hubby."

"Thanks girl. I don't know what he's up to but I'm liking it so far." Lovely smiled. Ryan was happy to see her in a good mood.

When they pulled up to the airport Lovey was excited. She knew her husband was the bomb but she didn't know they were leaving the state.

"Well get out, ya man is waiting over there for you." Ryan pointed at Phalon who was looking at Lovely with his hands extended. She smiled as she got out of the car and walked to him.

"Damn you look good!" Phalon took Lovely in his arms.

"Thank you."

"Look, I know we been going through it but I want us to be back the way we're supposed to be. I love you baby and I don't ever want to be without you again. I'm willing to do whatever I have to do to keep a smile on your face. I don't wanna ever be the cause of your tears." He kissed her lips.

"I love you to bae and I want us to be together too." They sealed their commitment with a kiss before boarding their jet to Vegas.

Asha was at home waiting for Rahsaan to come home. She needed him to explain why India was pregnant and she didn't know about it. She understood the fact that it happened while they were separated but he still should have kept it real with her.

Asha was sitting on the couch watching TV when Rahsaan came in.

"What's up ma?" Rah walked over and kissed her but she turned her head. Rahsaan was confused.

"Ok what did I do now, " he asked as he sat down next to her.

"India came over today."

Rahsaan heartbeat sped up. He knew he was fucked.

"Ok." He acted as if he didn't know why India would come over.

"Well she's pregnant; very pregnant and she says it's yours." She looked at him with the side eye.

"Whoa I don't know if that baby is mine."

"But you knew she was pregnant right," she asked.

"Yeah man." He finally said.

"So why haven't I heard about this before now, Rah? I thought we were doing better and now you're keeping shit like that from me. I mean, I know I fucked up but now your little girlfriend is having a baby around the same time as your wife." Asha was pissed.

"Look bae I'm sorry. I didn't mean for any of this shit to happen. I didn't tell you because we were trying to work out our problems. I didn't want anything coming between us."

"Well, I told the bitch to call us when she goes in labor. Then we'll do a DNA test, and if it's your baby, then we'll do the right thing but that bitch India better know her place because I have no problem putting her in it."

Rahsaan couldn't say anything because Asha was right and he wasn't about to lose his wife over India. They had been doing good and he wanted it to stay that way.

"Thanks for sticking by my side ma." He kissed her lips.

"I'm your wife, that's my job." Rahsaan smiled. He was happy that things worked out the way they did, all he had to do now was get Tracy to go away. He decided to ask Ryan for her help since it was her friend.

Chapter Twenty-Eight

3 Months later

Marco had been watching Lovely and he realized that it was time to move on. As much as he loved her he knew she'd never willingly be with him. He would have to accept loving her from afar. Plus, he asked around about Phalon and he wanted no parts of RBM. He started his car and pulled away from her house leaving behind the only woman he ever loved. He just wished he would have showed her how much he really loved her before it was too late.

Lovely and Phalon had been doing great. She even moved back into the house last week. Phalon knew in order to keep things good in his home he had to make his wife happy. So far so good.

"Aye bae I'm headed out but I won't be out too long." Phalon walked in the kitchen where Lovely was cooking.

"Ok bae be careful. I love you."

"Love you too ma." Phalon headed out. He was meeting the crew at Ace of Spades. He had to discuss what they were going to do with Lovely's brother. Phalon was a smart dude and he had been watching Stone watch him. Stone thought he was slick but Phalon was two steps ahead of him. He knew that was his wife's brother but he wasn't about to let him get away with shit.

Phalon was on his way to the club when he got a call from King.

"Yo"

"Man get over here to The Pink Kitty. This nigga Stone here high as fuck. He and Monte going at it." Phalon shook his head. He knew sooner or later they would have words.

"I'm on my way man." Phalon did a U-turn and headed to The Pink Kitty. When he pulled up he saw Monte in Stones face. Phalon got out leaving his car running. When he walked up he heard what they were arguing about.

"Nigga you beefing with me over some pussy that wasn't even yours to begin with? Anise is wifey and aint going nowhere, so get over it pot'nah." Monte was heated and couldn't believe Stone was coming at him sideways about his chick."

"Nigga what? You're new to the picture. I been around, " Stone countered.

"Yeah you been around but that one belongs to me my dude. So step the fuck out my face."

"Aye man let's go. Phalon grabbed Monte. "We don't need this shit right now. Too many witnesses and I know how you are." Monte knew Phalon was right so he walked away.

Pap! Pap! Pap!

Monte never saw it coming. He was ready to let the situation go but Stone was high and pissed. He pulled out his gun and shot Monte. Everything happened so fast that Phalon didn't know what happened until he saw his best friend lying on the ground bleeding. Shit had just got real.

Anise was sitting in a chair far away from everyone else. She wasn't talking to anyone and she couldn't stop crying. She couldn't believe it when Phalon had called her and told her Monte was shot. She still didn't know Stone was responsible. She hated that she had missed so much time with Monte. She wished she had made amends with him sooner. Now she was alone. He wasn't going to be here to rub her belly anymore. She cried harder when she realized that he wasn't going to be here for the birth of their son.

"This shit isn't fair!" She yelled.

Lovely felt bad for her friend. She walked over and tried to comfort her. She couldn't imagine losing Phalon.

"It's ok sis." Lovely didn't know what else to say.

"No it's not! Stop fucking acting like everything is ok! You have yo man. Mine is fighting for his life." Anise got up and walked away.

Lovely knew it was her emotions talking so she didn't take it to heart. She walked over to Phalon who seemed to be dealing with it. She really couldn't read his expression but she knew he was hurt. That was his best friend.

"Are you ok bae?" She rubbed his back.

"I'm good ma. I'm worried about Anise though. She loved that nigga to death."

"I know. I'm worried about her too."

Before anybody else could say anything the doctor walked out.

"The family of Monte Jones, " the doctor asked the crowd

Phalon along with everyone else stood up and waited to hear the news on Monte.

"So what's the deal?" Phalon didn't want to have to be the bearer of bad news to Monte's mom. She lived in Texas.

"Unfortunately, Mr. Jones was dead on arrival. We were unable to revive him."

Lovely was glad Anise had left out. She probably would have broken down upon hearing that.

"Thanks Doc." Phalon turned to everyone else.

"Babe I'm going to go be with Anise." Lovely hurried out of the waiting room to comfort Anise. She knew this was going to be tough for her friend.

"I'll call his mom and start the funeral preparations, " Phalon said and headed out in search of his wife and Anise. He didn't know how things was going to be without his Ace but he knew he had to be strong for Anise.

"Well I guess we better head out, " Rahsaan said. But before they had a chance to leave, Asha's phone rang. It was India.

"Hello?"

She was in labor.

"Ok we're on our way up, " Asha said. She had it where India had to call her and not her husband.

"What's up ma?" Rahsaan asked her.

"India is in labor. So let's go." They got on the elevator and headed to Labor and delivery.

When they got up there India was already pushing but there was another man by her side. Asha chuckled to herself as she and Rahsaan stood off to the side and watched. After fifteen minutes India delivered a 7pound 12 ounce baby boy that looked exactly like the guy standing next to her.

"Well I guess we're no longer needed here. India please don't call my husband ever again sweetie."

Asha took Rah's hand and walked out. It had been an eventful night. Rah was glad Ryan took care of Tracy too. He hadn't heard from her and that was a good thing. He was ready to live happy with his wife and kids. He had another son on the way and couldn't wait.

Chapter Twenty-Nine

The day of Monte's funeral was hard on everyone. Especially Anise. Here she was due any day and her other half was gone. She was glad Kyah was gone because she needed Aniyah with her. That was her daughter. No, she didn't birth her but she took care of her and loved her as if she did.

Anise sat in the front pew as the preacher spoke. Phalon was right next to her trying to comfort her. He knew how much Monte loved Anise. He still couldn't believe his boy was gone. Stone was Lovely's brother but that didn't mean shit anymore. He went against the grain when he killed Monte and now he had a price on his head.

Lovely barely heard a word the preacher said. Her mind was on her brother. She loved him dearly but she knew he was wrong. She felt stuck between her love for her brother and her loyalty for her husband and best friend. She knew if she chose Stone, she'd lose her family. But Stone was her family. He was there before everyone else but she had taken vows with Phalon. She had his children. And Anise was her best friend; her sister. She really didn't know what to do.

"Oh god no! Please bring him back!"

The preacher stopped and everyone turned their attention to the door. Lovely shook her head at Kyah making a scene. Kyah walked up to the casket and laid over it. She was crying so loud it sounded fake. When she was finally done she turned and saw Anise holding Aniyah.

"Give me my daughter!" She tried to take Aniyah from Anise.

"Bitch move!" Lovely got in her face and Phalon stood up to separate the two.

"This aint over. That's my child."

"Please, you haven't seen that baby in five months. Beat it because your presence is not wanted here."

"This shit aint over." Kyah laughed at Lovely.

She walked away and everyone turned back to the preacher who attempted to finish the eulogy. Not once did they notice the person sitting on the back pew with sunglasses and a hat on.

The rest of the funeral was a blur to Anise. All she wanted was Monte and he was gone. She knew life would be so different without him here.

The repass was at King's house. Anise wanted nothing to do with anyone. She stayed upstairs to herself the whole time. She was depressed and lost without Monte. Here she was due any day and he wouldn't be here to see their son come into the world. She didn't know how she'd cope. Monte was her everything and he was taken away from her. she laid in the bed and cried until she fell asleep.

Lovely hurt for her friend but she knew Anise was strong and would get through this. She thought back to when they first met Phalon and Monte. She smiled at the memories and how those two were inseparable. There would never be another like Monte.

"Rest in paradise brother." Lovely looked up to the sky.

Epilogue

Anise walked along the beach in Miami letting the sand engulf her feet. After a whole year she was finally at peace with Monte's death. Some days were better than others but she was dealing with it. Monte was gone but she still had a piece of him here. She had two beautiful kids and that was enough. Kyah had given up her rights to Aniyah and Anise adopted her. MJ was now walking and looking more like Monte every day.

"Come on sweet pea, let's get in the water." Anise grabbed MJ's hand. Aniyah was already by her side. She had taken to Anise as her mother and was attached to her hip. As they walked towards the water Aniyah took off running.

"Niyah get back here, " Anise yelled but her words fell on death ears. She picked MJ up and followed Aniyah but when she saw who Aniyah was running to she stopped dead in her tracks. She couldn't breathe.

"No this can't be real." She said to herself.

"Hey baby." Anise wanted to speak but her mouth wouldn't move. She just knew for sure she was dreaming. She was at his funeral. She watched them put him in the ground. She had cried over him so many nights. He wasn't there for the birth of their son. But here he was standing in the flesh.

"Come here ma." She walked towards him.

"How? I was at the funeral."

"I know and it's a lot I need to tell you but first I just want to see my kids and spend time with y'all." Anise couldn't stop the tears from falling. Just touching him confirmed that this was not a dream. Monte wasn't dead. He was here.

Anise had put the kids down for bed and now she was sitting here waiting for Monte to tell her the deal. What could possibly make him fake his death and leave her with two kids.

"Ok, so start talking and if I don't like what you have to say I'm shooting yo ass."

He laughed but quickly recoiled when he saw she wasn't in the mood for jokes.

"My bad baby. Well the bottom line is I had a hit out on me."

Anise was confused. Monte was part of one of the most ruthless brotherhoods around. Seeing her look of confusion he continued.

"When I first got in the game I was working for this cat named Luciano. He was an Italian mob boss. Well long story short when I hooked up with RBM I wanted no parts of them fucking Italians. Those muthafuckas crazy as hell. But I left on good terms or so I thought. I had dated Luciano's niece Bella and when I broke up with her she didn't take it too well. She had a hit out on me and I didn't know. Luciano of course sided with his niece. I wanted to be here to watch my kids grow up and marry you but I couldn't do that if I was six feet under. Long story short, I had to lay low and make them believe I was already dead until Ava took care of it. Now them Italian's are some bad muthafuckas but Harlem and King's sister is that bitch. She can make shit happen without a second thought." When Monte was done Anise was speechless.

"But Stone shot you" Anise was so confused.

"Look ma, I don't want to talk about that shit no more. I'm here with you and my kids and that's all that matters. I love you baby."

"I love you too."

Ring! Ring!

The ringing of the phone woke Anise up. She looked around the room and she was still in her bedroom not in Miami on the beach with Monte. This was the third time she had that dream this week. It seemed so real but she knew he was gone. She smiled at the picture of her and Monte that was sitting on the dresser. She didn't know what those dream were about but she felt like Monte was trying to tell her something. She got up to go check on her babies. Whoever had called hung up.

Aniyah was sleep so she went to MJ's room and he was sleep too. She closed the door and looked up. "We love you too baby."

THE END

Coming Soon from Demettrea

Black Scorpion

Prologue

"Don't fucking move or your brain will be splattered all over this fucking bed!" Reign held Eddie Johnson at gun point. He had literally been caught with his pants down. But that was how all her victims got caught up. Pussy will do it to you every time. Reign wasn't your average bad bitch. She had impeccable beauty that turned heads of both men and women. In her profession that was a plus.

Eddie was shaking so bad that he had pissed on his self. Here he was thinking he was about to sleep with a black goddess yet he was staring down the barrel of .357 magnum with a silencer. Never in his fifty-five years would he have thought this was how he'd die.

"Please I have money if that's what you want. You name the amount and it's all yours. I have a wife and kids." His pleas fell on deaf ears. In her profession Reign had developed a thick skin. She couldn't feel any remorse for her victims. She was paid very well to do a job and she wasn't leaving until it was done. She did her job so well she was nicknamed "Black Scorpion". Just like a scorpion, she caught her prey by surprise. Her beauty often paralyzed them. Once she got them where she wanted them she attacked.

"I don't need your money. I was sent here to do a job and that's what I'm going to do." Before Eddie could respond she let off two shots between his eyes killing him instantly.

After wiping down everything, making sure she left no traces of herself, she headed out. She got in her car and drove a few blocks away and took off her wig and changed her clothes. After getting out she drenched the inside with gasoline and lit a cigarette and threw the match in the car before running to the waiting car.

"Did everything go as planned?" Carla, her partner in crime and best friend asked.

"Smooth as butter baby. Now let's go get some rest. We got a big job in Atlanta this weekend. They sped off into traffic leaving no evidence that they ever were there.

CHAPTER ONE

K. Michelle was singing about getting a man and Reign was feeling it. It described her life to the fullest. She sat on the window ledge smoking a blunt. The life that she led didn't give her time for a relationship even though she craved it. The money was good but at the end of the day she was lonely.

I would give all this shit up just to stay home and be your wife. Fold some clothes give you what you like, boy you just don't know. She sang along with the song. She put out the blunt and closed the window. It was well after 1am and she had an early hair appointment in the morning. She laid down and thought about her life before she became a hit woman. It wasn't good but she longed for a normal life.

She thought back to when she caught her first body. She was seventeen and Roscoe, one of her mother's many boyfriends, called himself sneaking in her room. Reign knew her mom lived a party life. Tina always thought she was too young to be a mother. Reign wasn't even allowed to call her mom. Reign had started to develop early. So, when she turned seventeen, she was stacked like a grown woman which caused roaming eyes and eventually hands. She remembered it just like it was yesterday.

"What are you doing in my room Roscoe? I don't think my mom would like this."

Roscoe smiled showing off his gold tooth at the top. His salt and pepper beard was matted to his face and his breath reeked of alcohol. He was creeping Reign out as he moved closer to her bed, unbuckling his pants in the process. Reign sat in fear of what was about to take place. She always noticed the way he looked at her when her mother wasn't looking. She prayed to god that this was quick and fast. She thought about screaming for her mother but that would be useless. Her mother went to bed a while ago and was past drunk. Her pleas would go unheard. She tried to think of a happy time in her life.

"Now you just be a good little girl and I promise you I'll be gentle." He snatched off her pajama bottoms and licked his lips at her body. Reign was disgusted. After ripping her panties off he climbed on top of her and began kissing her earlobe, then her neck. Reign closed her eyes and silently cried. Why was God punishing her? She had been a good child even though her mother was shitty to her. She had good grades and she did everything her mother asked of her. Yet here she was getting her innocence taken by an old pervert. Before she knew what had happened Roscoe had pushed himself inside of her breaking the barrier that had never been broken. Reign cried. The pain was excruciating but she dealt with it.

A few humps later he pulled out and erupted all over her stomach.

"You did good, next time I'll teach you how to do some things." And just like that he left.

Reign rushed to the bathroom and threw up everything she had consumed that day. Once she was done she turned the shower on and let the water get as hot as she could stand it. She stepped in and scrubbed her skin until it was red. She couldn't believe that she was raped.

Reign laid in bed after scrubbing her body to rid herself of the shame. All she could think about was revenge and how she was going to get Roscoe back. She thought about Black Mike and how he always looked out for her. Yeah, she knew what she had to do. Roscoe had to go.

The next day Reign went to visit Black Mike at the chop shop he owned.

"Hey Mike." She spoke when she walked in. Big Mike was like a big brother to her. He was a few years older than her and took a liking to her because she wasn't like most girls from around the way.

"What's up lil' sis, " he greeted her. Big Mike was a big dude. He kind of put you in the mind of Rick Ross. He had a full beard like Rick and a big belly.

"I need a gun, " she said in a low tone but he heard her loud and clear. He grabbed her and pulled her into his office. After making sure the door was locked he turned to Reign.

"Start talking." He demanded. He didn't know what was going on but for her to ask for a gun he knew it was serious.

"I need a gun. That faggot ass nigga raped me. I want to take his life like he took mine." Big Mike was almost afraid to ask who. Reign had a dark look in her eyes that he had never saw before. He felt bad for whoever she wanted dead.

"Who raped you sis?" He was pissed. He felt it was too much pussy in the world for a nigga to take it.

"My mom's boyfriend. I want him dead." He didn't need to hear anymore.

"I tell you what, let me handle it. I'll come pick you up later. Until then just be cool. Don't say shit to nobody." Mike

was about to take Reign under his wing. He knew she could handle what he was about to throw her way and she would also know how to take care of herself in the future. He was about to mold her into a Boss Bitch.

Mike picked Reign up later that night. She didn't know where they were headed but she trusted Mike. He always looked out for her and it was never sexual. Even though Roscoe hadn't come over today she wanted to get out of the house. Everything about it reminded her of what happened the night before.

"So where we going," she asked as she bopped her head to Meek Mill.

"I got a surprise for you lil' sis. Just sit back and relax."

And she did just that. Thirty minutes later they pulled up to a pool hall. Reign was confused but went along with it. They walked in the pool hall and was greeted by a few of Mike's people

"Come on sis." He led her to the back and down the stairs to a metal door. When he got there he knocked three times. Someone opened the peephole and then they heard locks being undone. When they got in Reign was shocked to see Roscoe tied to a chair and gagged.

"Surprise sis. You asked for a gun to handle ya business but I had to make sure you did that shit right. I don't need you catching a bid behind this pervert. Here you go ma." He passed her a .357 magnum with a silencer attached.

"Now, I'm going to teach you how to shoot to kill. I don't want you to ever be in a situation like this again. Niggas like him don't deserve to live." He said pointing to Roscoe.

"Sincere, come over here and teach baby girl how to shoot."

There was a practice target on the wall. It was like their own personal gun range. Reign looked at the person he called Sincere and almost choked. She had never seen someone so fine in her life. Her body started to feel things she was unfamiliar with.

Sincere walked up behind Reign and took hold of her hands. He showed her how to stand and how to aim at her target.

"Ok lil' mama. You ready to take ya first shot?" Sincere asked.

She nodded. Most young girls probably would have been nervous but not Reign. She felt her adrenaline rushing as she prepared to shoot the gun for the first time.

"Ok, on the count of three I want you to try shooting the target." Sincere counted to three as he backed away from Reign. When he reached three she took her first shot and hit the target right on.

"Oh shit! Lil' sis you a natural." Mike boasted.

Before anyone else could respond Reign turned to Roscoe and put a bullet right between his eyes. Mike as well as everyone else in the room was taken back. Her first body was a one shot kill and she had no feelings about it. She sat the gun down and turned to Mike.

"Can you take me home so I can shower please? That nigga's blood splattered all on my shirt." Sincere couldn't believe how gangster she was. That actually turned him on but the fact that she was young is what held him back. He was twenty-two and didn't have time to be caught up with a young

chick. Plus he had a girl at home. That day Black Scorpion was born.

Reign climbed in bed, alone as usual and tried to get some sleep. Thoughts of Sincere plagued her mind. She had always had a crush on him since that day she saw him in the pool hall but he had a girl. They always flirted back and forth but it never went beyond that. They worked together and that was a line she didn't cross. She felt like she would be betraying Big Mike if she dated inside the crew. "In another lifetime." She thought as she closed her eyes.

CHAPTER TWO

Sincere Williams was that dude. From his pretty boy swag to the labels he wore. Everything about him screamed "Boss". He stood 6 feet even and had dark skin that was without blemish. He kept his hair cut low and had waves. He had a cocky attitude and you couldn't tell him that he wasn't the shit. At twenty-five he was a well-established business man. He had survived being in the game without doing any fed time or being killed. He was blessed. He wasn't like most hustlers that stayed in the game. He did what he had to, to come up and he invested his money. Now fast forward five years later he was a rich man. He invested in stock, as well as owned a clothing store, a recording studio and a club. All he did was sit back and collect money while he had others working for him. He was living the good life. Not to mention he had a bad bitch on his arm, even though he craved Reign. While Jaleesa was bad as in cute and stacked, Reign was bad in every sense of the word. She had a body to die for, she was cute and she was street smart. Most importantly she understood the struggle. Jaleesa was a good girl and frowned upon Sincere's crew. Jaleesa was born with a silver spoon in her mouth and was spoiled. Sincere loved her but he wasn't in love with her.

Sincere walked in the pool hall for a meeting that Big Mike had called. Big Mike was a mentor to Sincere. He had put him on when he was a young cat with nothing and for that Sincere would forever be grateful.

"What's up Sin?" Candy, a bar maid called out. It wasn't a secret that she liked him but he wasn't fucking with her. He didn't do any chick. He only fucked with bad bitches, not that Candy wasn't cute but she had three kids and three different daddies. Sincere stayed away from shit like that.

"What up Candy." He spoke and kept it moving. He made his way downstairs where everyone was waiting.

"What up fam, " he greeted as he walked in the door.

"What's up?" Big Mike greeted. He loved Sincere like a son and he was proud of the man he had become.

"Hey Sin." Reign spoke. He smiled.

"What's good baby girl." She smiled back. Mike thought it was cute how the two flirted.

"Now that everyone is here let's get started. First off, I want to tell Reign that she did good on the Eddie Johnson job. Check your account, you should be well compensated for it. Also, Sincere I need you to get together a team for the blocks we have on the east side. I know you are done with this side of the business but I don't trust them other knuckle heads to put together a strong team. I want Ramone in charge so do what needs to be done and then report back to me. I will be on vacation with the wife next week so you are in charge. Anything they need has to go through you."

Sincere shook his head in understanding. Unbeknown to either of them was the scowl Mike Jr. wore. Never mind that Mike Jr. was irresponsible and a hot head. He thought he should have been second in command after his dad, not Sincere.

"I gotchu boss," Sincere replied.

"Well meeting adjourned, and Reign take some time off and do something fun. Sincere see to it that she doesn't do another job for a while. You have more than enough money to chill for a minute."

Reign was fine with that. "Ok Mike." She replied.

"I got her Mike." Sincere winked at Reign.

She put up the middle finger as she stood to leave. Sincere followed behind her admiring her backside. Yeah she was a bad bitch. Reign only stood at 5'6 and maybe about 135 pounds. She had a mocha colored complexion and she kept her hair laid. Sincere liked the fact that she didn't wear make-up. Maybe a little gloss but that was all.

"Wait up ma." He called after her as she exited the pool hall.

"What's up Sin?" He loved when she called him Sin. It sounded sexy coming off her lips. Lips that he wanted to kiss.

"What you doing tonight ma?" He wanted her to chill with them at Epiphany. His boy Phalon was hosting a White Party.

"Not a damn thing." She answered.

"Well come chill with a nigga tonight." Reign thought about it and realized she had nothing to do.

What the hell. She thought. "Cool, what time are you picking me up?" She asked.

"Be ready about nine ma, " he responded.

"Ok cool." She turned to walk to her car but he grabbed her in his arms.

"You know I'm gone make you mine right?" He whispered in her ear.

"Boy please. What about Jaleesa?" She tried to pull from his embrace but he didn't let go.

"What about her? It's you that I want ma?" She looked in his eyes and saw that he was serious. She was nervous. She was in love with him but they had never crossed that line. She never really dated. Maybe a few here and there but nothing too serious.

"Sin, move. I have to get dressed for tonight. He held on to her a little longer before kissing her forehead.

"Ok ma. Be ready on time." She turned to walk away and he smacked her on the ass.

"You play too much Sin." She acted as if she was mad but she liked the attention that she was getting from him. Even though they flirted all the time, it was different now. She got in the car with a smile on her face.

It was 8:35 and Reign had just got out the shower. She had about thirty minutes before Sincere arrived. She grabbed her clothes from the closet which consisted of and all white Gucci pantsuit with the back out. She chose some all-white gladiator heels and gold accessories to complete her outfit. Just as she was putting on her shoes there was a knock on the door. She headed to the answer it and when she opened it her mouth dropped. Sincere was fine but he was looking good enough to eat right now.

"Hey Sin, let me grab my purse and we can go."

Before she could walk away he pulled her in his arms and kissed her. Surprised by his actions she pulled away but he didn't make it easy for her. She finally gave in. they kissed for a good minute before he pulled back.

"Damn yo lips soft as hell"

Reign walked away to grab her purse. She didn't know what to say about that kiss but she liked it. *Jaleesa who?* she thought. When she walked back into the living room Sincere was waiting at the door.

"You look good ma." He said as he ushered her out the door.

CHAPTER THREE

Sincere walked in Epiphany hand in hand with Reign. He felt good; he had a bad bitch on his arm and he was looking good. He ignored the glares from women as they made their way to VIP. His boy Phalon had them set up real nice.

"You want a drink ma?" Sincere asked once they had reached their booth.

"Yeah, get me a Ciroq and lime juice." He flagged the waitress down and ordered her drink as well as a bottle of Ace.

"So where's wifey and why didn't you bring her with you tonight?" Reign asked in a sarcastic tone. She liked Sincere but she wasn't stupid.

"Look are we gone have a good time or talk about Jaleesa all night?"

"My bad, did I hit a soft spot?" He smirked. That's what he liked about Reign, she didn't back down just because he said so. She had her own voice unlike Jaleesa. Jaleesa went with whatever he said. She was like a puppet he controlled. He hated a weak woman.

"Nah ma, but I just want to enjoy the night with you." He scooted closer to her and wrapped his arm around her waist.

"Don't get too comfy nigga. You fine and all but fact remains you have a bitch at home." Reign shot.

"Yo mouth is reckless, " he said, still not moving his arms from around her.

"You like it though."

"Hell yeah."

"Come on, I wanna dance." She got up and he followed. He wasn't much of a dancer but if that's what she wanted, fuck it. Diced Pineapples blared throughout the club as Reign danced on Sincere. He stood there with his hands on her waist enjoying the show. He watched her move and wondered how she'd be in bed. By the end of the song his dick was hard and he knew she felt it. He walked her off the dance floor and back to the booth. He sat down and then sat her on his lap.

"See what you did?" he asked referring to his hard on.

"She looked at him and smiled before trying to get up but he pulled her back down.

"You know I'm gone make you mines eventually right?"

"That's what ya mouth say but we'll see."

He held on to her and nibbled on her ear. She let a soft moan escape her lips and that turned him on even more. He slipped his hand down her pants and felt how wet she was.

"See how wet you are, " he, asked taking his hand out and licking his finger.

"Boy move." She got up and he didn't stop her this time.

"Don't be mad cause we on the verge of fucking right here in the club." He retorted.

"Nigga please, aint nobody about to fuck you." She walked away and he just smiled. He knew he was wearing her down. He just had to take care of the situation at home and he was coming for his queen.

They partied well into the wee hours.

"Here ma can you drive? A nigga gone for real." She took the keys from him and they retrieved the car from valet.

"Damn I always wanted to drive this car." Reign admired the all black Maserati as she climbed in the driver's seat.

"All you had to do was ask ma, " he said as he got comfortable in the passenger seat. The twenty-minute drive to Reign's apartment took them less than fifteen because she was pushing the Maserati. She fell in love with the car and vowed to get one soon. When they pulled up Reign got out and headed to the door with Sincere following close behind. Before she could even open the door he had his hands around her waist kissing the back of her neck.

"Move Sin." She said even though she didn't want him to move.

"I can't help it, you look so fucking good ma." He let go of her long enough to close the door. She used that opportunity to walk away but wasn't quick enough. He pulled her back to him and kissed her. He kissed her with so much passion. After a few minutes of making out she pushed him away and walked towards her room.

"Why you playing games ma?" He asked

"You have loose ends to tie up player before you can rock with me." She tried to close her door but he caught it.

"Well can I lay next to you then at least?"

"Nope, there's a pillow and blanket in the hall closet. Goodnight." She closed the door in his face and he was pissed. He was horny as hell but Reign didn't care. There was no way she was resulting to being a side chick. If Sincere wanted her then he had to come correct.

CHAPTER FOUR

Reign was happy for the opportunity to lounge around the house. Usually she was on the go doing jobs. She laid in bed catching up on her Vh1 shows. It was still fairly early. She hadn't spoken to Sincere in two days but that was normal with him. She was halfway through Love and hip hop Atlanta when she heard a knock at the door. She paused the DVR and headed down the hall to the door. She looked through the peephole and saw Sincere's fine ass. Reign thought about making him wait while she put on some clothes, because all she had on was boy shorts and a sports bra. Fuck it. She opened the door.

"Hey Sin, " she spoke. He didn't respond. Instead he pulled her in his arms.

"What's good lil' mama?" He asked as he let her go.

"Just chilling. What brings you by?"

"I just wanted to see you before I went out of town this weekend." Sincere closed the door and followed her to the bedroom. Reign climbed back in bed and Sincere took off his shoes and climbed in next to her.

"Why do women watch this garbage?" He referred to reality TV.

"It's entertainment."

"I bet." He pulled her close to him and held her. She didn't protest. She was in love with Sincere and tired of pretending.

Reign woke up in Sincere's arm. She looked over at the clock and it read 3:45 am. She got up to go to the bathroom and Sincere woke up.

"Where you going, " he asked as he sat up.

"Chill Pa, I'm going to the bathroom."

Sincere laid back down and waited for her. He didn't know why he was so gone over a girl that wasn't even his but he was. When he first met her two years ago he knew it was something about her.

When Reign came back she climbed in bed facing Sincere.

"Sin."

"Huh?" He responded never opening his eyes.

"Why do you want me so much? I mean you got a bitch at home that you've been with for a minute, yet you're in my bed." Reign needed to know what his intentions were because she wasn't playing second to no bitch. Sincere opened his eyes and looked at her.

"You're smart, you don't take no shit from me and you fine as hell. I know that your heart is pure, you don't have ulterior motives and you got yo own. You the type of chick to ride for her nigga. I don't know how I fell for yo little ass but I did and the shit won't go away." He said honestly.

Reign kissed him. Nothing too sensual but a peck. Sincere was still looking in her eyes. "I'm in love with you Sin but you have a bitch at home and I can't rock like that." She admitted.

"I feel you ma and I'd never hurt you intentionally. That shit at home is already a wrap so you don't need to worry about that." He assured her.

"I don't want no bullshit from ol' girl Sin."

"I got you ma." He kissed her lips while his hands roamed her body. Reign was wet and horny. She hadn't had sex in six months and was more than ready. Sincere climbed on top of her.

"You love me right?" He asked her.

"Yes." She replied. He kissed her with so much passion. Reign didn't know whether she was coming or going. If she could feel like that from just a kiss, then what would the sex do to her? Sincere lifted her sports bra above her head. He licked and sucked both nipples showing each one special attention. Reign cried out. He had her gone and they hadn't even had sex yet. Sincere made his way all the way down her body. He kissed her belly button and made his way between her legs. He kissed the insides of her thighs as he pulled her boy shorts off. He dove head first into her wetness and that really sent Reign over the edge. He licked, sucked and bit on her clit.

"Ooh shit, Sin." She was grabbing the back of his head. Sincere inserted a finger in her pussy while he ate it.

"Shit Sin, I'm about to cum!" She cried out. That made him work faster. Her legs shook and all her juices leaked right in his mouth. He kissed her pussy again before climbing on top of her.

"I love you Reign. I have loved you since the first time I saw you two years ago." He confessed. He stood up and took his clothes off before climbing back on top of her. He teased her clit with the head, rubbing all over her opening. Reign got bold and grabbed his dick and guided it in her. They were both so caught in the moment that neither bothered to use protection.

Sincere moved slow and steady inside her. She wasn't just any female. He wasn't fucking her. He was making love to her mind and her body. This was only the beginning but all good things must come to an end, right?

CHAPTER FIVE

"So, Tina what's a fine chick like yourself doing in Cali?" Clint asked Reign not knowing she was using her alias. He didn't know that he was about to die either. He was so caught up in thinking he was about to get some pussy that he let his guard down.

"A new start. I went through so much at home that I needed to get away." Tina replied.

"Well you've come to the right place baby. I got you ma, " he said. Reign smiled at how naïve he was. She didn't feel sorry for him at all because he was supposed to be this big time hustler and here he was about to fall victim to some pussy he'd never get. Clint was a pimp with a stable of twelve girls. One of the girls Lisa was only sixteen and her sister felt some kind of way about him pimping her little sister. She didn't have much money but she knew that Black Scorpion could get the job done. Reign took on the job for her own personal reasons, not for the money. She hated men that used and abused women, especially young girls. Clint thought he had another lost young girl to add to his stable. He would soon learn the hard way.

Clint got Reign, or Tina as he knew her to leave the bar with him. He was stupid enough to take her to his house. Mistake number two. The first being, he trusted a female with a big ass and pretty smile.

"Make yourself at home baby. Daddies gonna take care of you from here on out."

Reign laughed in her head. *This stupid muthafucka has no idea. She thought.* After a few hours of talking and drinks Clint was tipsy. He never saw the pill that Reign put in his drink. He was now feeling the effects of the pill. He tried to stand but the room was spinning.

"You bitch! What did you do to me, " he asked as he fell back on the bed. No one was in the house but them two. He housed his girls at a different house. He now regretted bringing her here. Reign pulled out her .357 with the silencer and walked right up to him.

"So you like pimping little girls huh?" he was so out of it from the pill that he couldn't respond. Reign laughed and then put the gun between his eyes and pulled the trigger. She didn't have to worry about her fingerprints being on anything because the tips were fake. She left quietly and undetected.

Reign stretched as she sat up in the bed. It had been a long night but it was well worth it. No amount of money would have made her change her mind about killing Clint. She hated men that prayed on young girls. Reign headed to the bathroom to take care of her hygiene. Today she planned on doing some retail therapy. She loved being able to provide for herself. She didn't need a man to validate her. All though she loved to have one around to cuddle with and to make sweet love to her. She was in love with Sincere but she knew he wasn't ready for her. He came with too much baggage.

After washing her face and brushing her teeth she grabbed her phone and headed to the kitchen to grab a bite to eat.

Reign's place was bad ass. Everything in her living room was all white and being that she rarely had company and she didn't have kids, it was easy to keep it that way. Her kitchen had state of the art appliances, all of which were stainless steel. She had granite countertops and her walls were red. Reign was happy with her accomplishments. He was set financially for the rest of her life; mainly because she didn't splurge unnecessarily. She knew how to save and invest her money so if she wanted to she could retire from being a hit woman. That was actually something that had been on her mind lately.

The ringing of her phone brought her out of her thoughts.

"Hello?" She answered as she opened the refrigerator.

"Hey sexy. What you doing?" It was Sincere. That put a smile on her face.

"Nothing, about to fix something to eat. What's up with you?"

"Aint shit. Just thought about you."

"How cute."

"Yeah aight. Keep being a smart ass. But I gotta go, I may stop through there later."

"Ok." They hung up.

Reign didn't know why she was entertaining the thought of being with Sincere when he had a girl. She wasn't into being a side chick by any means. She knew she had to stop whatever this was they were doing before it got out of hand.

Chapter Six

Jaleesa laid in bed waiting for Sincere to come home. This was beginning to be a regular thing and she didn't know what was up with him. She loved him but he was starting to show her his ass and she wasn't the one. He thought Jaleesa was naïve but she was far from it. If he wanted to play games then she was ready to play right along with him.

She knew exactly why he was acting the way he was.............Reign. Jaleesa hated her with a passion. Sincere was always sniffing behind her and Jaleesa was tired of it.

"His ass wanna play!" Jaleesa got up and got dressed. It was after midnight and she wasn't going to be here when Sincere decided to walk his ass in the house. She was going to beat him at his own game.

When Sincere walked in the house it was after 2am. He headed to the bedroom that he shared with Jaleesa only to find it empty. He knew she was probably at her parent's house. Whenever she called herself mad at him she'd leave and go to her parent's house. Sincere was actually glad that she was gone so he didn't have to deal with the nagging. He had a long day and just wanted to rest.

As he laid across the bed thoughts of being deep inside Reign invaded his mind. She was perfect for him in every way. She was like the female version of him. She matched his fly. He wanted to leave Jaleesa but he felt loyalty to her. He was in love with Reign and knew he had to do something quick. It was only so much Reign would put up with.

"Fuck this shit!" Sincere got up and headed out the door. He needed to be with Reign. He had a long day and needed to be in her presence.

When he pulled up to Reign's house he texted her and told her to open the door. When she opened the door she was wearing boy shorts and a tank top.

"Damn ma, you trying to make a nigga catch blue balls." He said looking at her.

"Whatever nigga." She turned and walked back to her room and he followed. She climbed in bed while he stripped out of his clothes. He climbed in the bed with her and pulled her close.

"Damn I missed you." He inhaled her scent.

"Is that right?" She replied sarcastically.

"Don't get fucked up Reign." He replied as his hands roamed her body.

"By who? You must have forgotten that I'm nice with mines." He flipped her over and climbed on top of her.

"What's all that shit you talking?" He kissed her lips and then her neck.

"Huh? You quiet now." He bit her nipple through her shirt.

"Move boy." She playfully pushed him away. He kissed her lips.

"I love you Reign." He confessed as he look in her eyes. She knew he was telling the truth and she felt the same way.

"I love you too." That was all it took for Sincere. That night he made love to her like it was their last time together.

Rain woke up to the sound of her phone. She looked at the clock and it read 3:15 am. Sincere was sleep next to her like he had been for the last few nights.

"Hello?" She answered with annoyance in her voice. She didn't know who had the nerve to call her at this hour.

"Could you please tell my man to bring his ass home?"

"Excuse me. Who is this?"

"Jaleesa. Now can you tell Sincere he has thirty minutes to get home and trust he don't want to fuck with me." Jaleesa hung up and Reign looked at her phone in disbelief. She couldn't believe that Jaleesa had the balls to call her phone. Even more she couldn't believe Sincere. She had told him from jump she didn't do drama and he assured her that he and Jaleesa were through. He had lied to her and she was pissed that she let her feelings get involved. She smacked him in the head.

"What the fuck!" He sat up trying to figure out what Reign was tripping about.

"Get the fuck up and get out nigga. And tell yo bitch to stop calling my damn phone." She got out the bed and walked out. Sincere was confused. He got up and went after her.

"What the fuck is yo problem Reign?" He asked.

"Niggas like you. You aint shit Sin." She sat on the couch trying not to cry. She wasn't supposed to get her feelings involved. She knew niggas wasn't shit yet she let her guard down with Sincere.

"What the fuck did I do?" He was still confused.

"You still with Jaleesa nigga but you in my bed, " she shouted."

"Man that's what you tripping about? I aint with that girl. I'm here with you."

"Get the fuck out Sin!" He knew he was wrong. He wasn't with Jaleesa physically but had never actually broke up with her either. She knew too much shit about him and he couldn't chance her snitching on him. He took one last look at Reign before walking away. He had to figure out a way to fix this because he needed Reign in his life. She was his heart.

After he got dressed Sincere headed out. Before he walked out the door he took one last look at Reign and he felt like shit. He walked out her house and her life. He just hoped it wasn't for good.

<><><><>

Reign hadn't talked to Sincere in almost two weeks. She ignored all his calls and didn't answer her door. She was heartbroken and nothing was helping. She was sitting at home drinking wine and listening to music. Sevyn Streeter was blasting through the sound system and it described her and Sincere to the tee.

Don't know how you do to me, what you do, But baby, ooh you. You do it so good and yeah we break up. I break all your stuff that's just how we love. We keep it so hood. How you make me feel, can't nobody do that for me and we go through some things But I can't stop loving you And oh I like it, I like it Oh I like it, I like it Oh I like it, I like it Oh I like it, I like it The way my body feels when you laying right beside me. Boy I'm a be right here. Don't care what nobody say, cause oh I like it, I like it.

She missed Sincere and almost called him but she had to be strong. It was time to move on. He had a bitch at home.

"Fuck this shit man." Reign got up and headed to her room. She was going out and having fun. She wasn't about to sit at home and mope around. Fuck Sincere. She thought. As she picked out her outfit she called Carla to see if she wanted to go out.

"Hey chica. What you doing?"

"Nothing girl. What's up?"

"Let's hit up Sphinx. I need to get out this damn house."

"I'm down with it. You driving?

"That's cool. Be ready in an hour." She hung up and headed to the shower.

When Carla and Reign walked in the club it was hype. Reign headed to the bar to get a drink.

"Let me get a Red Berry Ciroq with lime juice." She ordered.

She bopped her head to the music and unbeknown to her she was being watched. After waiting a few minutes for her drink she grabbed it and headed to the dance floor where Carla was.

"It's live as hell in here girl." Carla was hyped and Reign just laughed as she swayed her hips to the beat. She was in her own zone never noticing the eyes that were watching her.

Rico was mesmerized by the female dancing on the floor. He had made up in his mind that he had to get her number. It was something about her. She had an exotic look and her body was banging.

"Damn shorty bad as fuck." Dame, Rico's right hand said as he saw what his boy was looking at.

"Hell yeah. I want her." He looked at Dame. Dame knew what to do.

"Say no more." He guzzled down his drink and headed out of the VIP section towards Reign. When he reached her, he tapped her on the shoulder.

"Excuse Ms. Lady, my man Rico wanted to know if you'd join him in VIP." Dame pointed to Rico. Reign's eyes followed his finger. He was definitely fine.

"Sure." She smiled at Rico as he watched her. She looked around for Carla to tell her where she was going but Carla was nowhere in sight. Dame led the way and she followed.

"This is Rico." Dame introduced before walking away.

"So Rico, why is it that you couldn't introduce yourself to me? You had to send your boy over."

"Sweetheart it's not that simple. A man of my stature can't has to be very careful. I have people that want my spot and I can't make it easy for them." Reign wanted to know who this man was. He seemed to be someone of importance.

"So what is your name?" he asked her.

"Reign."

He smiled. "I like that. So tell Reign, are you single?"

"Very much so." Reign didn't know what it was about Rico but his demeanor screamed *I'm that nigga.*

Rico and Reign chilled until the club was closing, getting to know each other. Rico knew without a doubt he had to have her in every way possible. He could tell that Reign was a bad bitch and he needed her on his arm.

"Well it was nice chilling with you Rico."

"Likewise baby." He pulled her in his arms and whispered in her ear.

"Come home with me." Reign smiled.

"No." Rico wasn't used to a woman telling him no.

"Alright ma. Well can can I see you again, " he asked her.

"Call me and we'll work something out." She stepped from his embrace and walked towards her car.

"Damn she bad as hell, " Rico said grabbing his dick. He knew without a doubt he was cuffing her.

Chapter Seven

Rico Hernandez was what you called a Don. He was simply the man. Nothing on the east coast went down without him knowing. He was destined to be a man of power. He didn't asked for it, it was sort of inherited. His great grandfather Armando Hernandez started and organization of drugs and weapons. Whatever you needed they could supply.

Fast forward years later and now Rico was in charge. He was what most called a pretty boy. He had smooth almond colored skin, curly black hair that he kept cut close. He stood at 5'11 and was 200 pounds with muscles ripping from everywhere. He stayed in the gym to keep up his shape and women loved him but he was looking for the one. The one to give the Hernandez name to; the one to bear his seeds. When he first laid eyes on Reign he was beyond infatuated. It was something about her that stood out and he wanted her. He didn't give a damn if she was already taken.

It had been exactly a week since he met her. Due to business he hadn't been able to talk to her but today he was going to make it a point to do so. He dialed her number and waited as the phone rang.

"Hello?" Her voice was soothing.

"Well, hello Ms. Reign." Reign had thought he forgot about her. She waited all week for his call and she didn't have his number.

"Hi to you."

"I know it took me a minute to call but I had business to handle. So can I take you out to dinner tonight."

"We can do dinner." She gave him her address and hung up. Rico was excited about seeing her. He hadn't been this infatuated with a girl since his wife Kendra died. He just hoped he wasn't getting in too deep with her. He made a mental note to do a background check on her.

It was a little after nine when Reign heard someone at the door. She grabbed her purse and headed to the door. It was a short white man.

"Can I help you, " she asked when she opened the door.

"Yes, I am your driver for the evening. I will be driving you to dinner with Mr. Hernandez."

Reign was impressed. Rico was doing it big. She locked up the door and followed the driver to the limo that awaited.

Twenty minutes later they pulled up to a huge mansion. Reign thought they were going out but it seemed as if Rico had other plans so she just rolled with it.

The driver opened the door for her and led her up the walk way where she was met by Rico at the door.

"Glad you could make it." Rico took Reign in his arms and hugged her. She inhaled his Armani cologne. She couldn't help but think how much of a boss this nigga was.

"Thanks for having me." She followed him to the dining room and he pulled her chair out for her.

"What do you wanna drink ma?"

"Ciroq and lime juice if you have it."

"He nodded to their server who went to get her drink.

"So Ms. Reign why is it a woman as fine as you on the market?"

"Well, I haven't found the right man to change that."

"Damn, must be my lucky night because I plan on changing that." Reign smiled. She was far from naïve but he was smooth with his.

"We shall see." The server brought her drink and they continued getting to know each other. By the time dinner was served Rico was even more intrigued with her.

Rico cut his steak and fed her from his plate. Reign thought it was cute. By the time they were done eating Reign was hot. She was so horny and turned on by him that if he tried to sleep with her tonight she would.

"Let's go to the den and chill." He took her hand and led her to the den were he turned on some music. They sat on the couch and kicked it some more.

"Stay with me tonight." He asked. Reign was tired of playing it safe so she threw caution to the wind.

"Ok." She replied. Rico leaned over and kissed her lips and she accepted. They kissed for what seemed liked forever before Rico pulled away.

"Come on, let's go upstairs. I wanna give you a massage, pamper you like you deserve." She took his hand that was held out and followed him upstairs. His bedroom was the size of her living room and dining room put together. It had a fire place, 70 inch TV mounted on the wall and a balcony where you could see the pool area outside. It was decorated in black and white and his bed was huge. Reign had money but she was impressed with his style.

"Go ahead and get comfortable ma. It's some t-shirts in that top drawer. I'll be right back." He walked out the room and she grabbed one of his t-shirts and changed. Reign climbed in the bed and waited for Rico to come back. A few minutes later he came back with a glass of wine for her and some oils.

"Lay on ya stomach ma and get comfortable." She laid down and he climbed on the bed and started massaging her. Reign was in heaven. She never had a man be so attentive to her and she was enjoying it.

After a good hour Reign was relaxed. Ric had massaged every part of her body and she loved it.

"Damn that felt so good." She was now lying on her back looking at him. He leaned down and kissed her lips.

"I'm glad." Reign pulled him back to her and kissed his lips. He pulled her in his arms and let his hands roam all over her body. His dick was rock hard and he wanted her. He didn't expect to get it so soon but he was ready. Rico pulled her on top of him.

"I want you ma, " he said to her. She smiled and got off of him. She pulled the shirt off revealing her black lace bra and thong.

"Damn." He replied. He stood up and took off his clothes and then walked to Reign who was now standing naked. Her body was perfect. Rico took her in his arms and kissed her with so much passion. Both knew after tonight nothing would be the same. He wanted her in every sense.

"I wanna see what you can do ma." He let her go and got back in bed. He motioned for her to climbed on top and she did. Rico guided her hips making her pussy rub the tip of his dick. Reign moaned in pleasure. Just the sensation drove her crazy. Rico wasn't huge but he wasn't small either and he was quite thick. Finally he let her slide down on his pole and she took it like a pro. Reign moved her hips slowly and Rico was loving how tight her pussy was. Yeah he could definitely get used to this.

"Ride that shit ma." He smacked her on the ass and that made her go faster. Reign was in her own world.

"I want you to cum all on my dick." She didn't respond. Smack!

He smacked her ass again. "You here me?"

"Yes."

"Yes what?" He asked.

"Ooh shit! Yes daddy! I'm about to cum." He guided her hips.

"Cum for daddy." And she did.

"Shit Rico!" he flipped her over on her stomach and she tooted her ass in the air. He entered her from the back and beat it up. Reign came yet again. She had never had sex so explosive. Sincere wasn't no slouch but Rico was that deal.

"Shit I'm about to cum ma." Rico pulled out and shot his load on her ass. He couldn't believe he had a bad bitch and her sex game was on point. Yeah he was cuffing her. Fuck the rest, she was it.

"You know you mine's now." He joked but was serious.

"Look at you staking claim." She joked back.

"Well let's see where this goes but I do like you Reign."

"I like you too Rico."

Chapter Eight

Reign had been kicking it with Rico for a few weeks now. He was everything she wanted in a man. She hadn't talked to Sincere in a few weeks and she was fine with that. He had lied to her and that hurt. She really care about him but he showed her his true colors and now she had moved on with Rico.

Today was a chill day for her. She had just did a job last night and didn't have another one lined up. Rico was out of town and Carla was booed up. It was just her, ratchet TV and popcorn. She was watching the Love and hip hop Atlanta reunion when her dor bell sounded. She got up to answer it and was surprised to see Sincere.

"Hey Sin. What are you doing here?" He just grabbed her and kissed her. She pushed him away.

"Stop Sin." He looked at her with puppy dog eyes.

"I took care of that situation. I need you ma." He tried to grab her again only to be pushed away.

"It's too late Sin."

"Come on ma. I fucked up but I took care of it. I'm sorry. Don't do this to me."

"Sin, I have a man." That broke his heart. He never thought she'd move on that fast.

"No, don't do this Reign." She didn't respond. Sincere took her in his arms. She tried to pull away but he didn't let her this time. He kicked the door closed with his foot and walked her to the wall.

"Do you love him?" She turned her head and he turned it back.

"Look at me and tell me you don't love me and I'll leave you alone." He said but she couldn't say that because she did love him. It didn't change the fact that she was with Rico though. She had cared about Rico too but Sin hurt her and she couldn't forgive that.

"Let me go Sin." He smiled. She still loved him. He kissed her and grouped her body. She tried to push him away but her body said something different. He pulled her jogging pants down while he was still kissing her. He noticed that she didn't have on any panties. He fingered her. She was wet and horny. She knew she should have stopped him but her heart took over.

Sincere pulled his dick out and inserted it in her.

"You still love me ma?" She shook her head yes and he took that as his cue to leave his mark in her.

"Shit you wet as fuck!" She didn't respond. It felt good but she was still hurt. A tear fell down her face but they still kept going.

"I fucking love you girl." Sincere proclaimed as he came in her. He pulled out of her and she slid to the floor and cried. Sincere sat next to her.

"Don't cry ma."

"Get out Sin. We shouldn't have done this." He tried to pull her to him.

"No Sin! Please leave. We can't do this shit no more." He didn't say anything else. He got up and fixed his clothes and left.

Reign felt bad for sleeping with Sincere when she was with Rico. They hadn't defined what they were but they did everything a couple did and when he introduced her it was as his girl. She was glad he was out of town because she couldn't face him right now. Not after what she just did. He was too good to her and she knew she couldn't go there with Sincere again.

Reign sat on the floor for quite some time after Sincere left. She wasn't supposed to be caught in her feelings like this. She always portrayed this hard interior and now here she was falling apart over a man that she have never been with in the first place. But the heart want's what it want's right?

Chapter Nine

Rico had just got back in town and all he could think about was Reign. He couldn't get enough of her. She was like a breath of fresh air. She was everything he wanted in a woman. He was ready to take that next step with her. They had only been together a few weeks but who put's a time frame on love? He wanted her to be the first thing he woke up to and the last thing he saw before he went to bed. He knew she had her own money but he wanted to spoil her.

He told his driver to take him to her house. He needed to see her before he went home. The week he was away was the worst and he decided net time he'd bring her along. When they pulled up to her house her car was parked in the driveway. He grabbed the bags that he had for her and headed to the door. After ringing the bell he waited and she answered a few seconds later.

"What's up ma?" She smiled when she saw him.

"Hey you. When did you get back in town?" She moved aside for him to come in.

"Just now. I wanted to see you before I headed home. A missed yo little ass." He pulled her in his arms.

"Aww. I missed you too."

"Here this is for you." He passed her the two bags he had.

"You didn't have to bring me anything." She looked in the bags and she had two pair of Red Bottom's and three jewelry boxes.

"I know but I like spoiling you." She opened the first box and it was a pair of diamond earrings. The second box was a necklace with a diamond encrusted heart. The third box was a car key. Reign was confused.

"What the hell is this Rico?" she held the key up. He smiled.

"Well you said how much you liked maserati's so I got you one. I mean I ride nice, I look nice so it's only right that my girl match my fly. Anything you need ma I got you. I know you got ya own and I admire that about you. Hell that only makes me want to do for you even more." She smiled.

"Thanks bae." She hugged him.

"Anything for you ma. We can go pick up your car tomorrow. I need to get home cause I'm tired as hell."

"Aww you're leaving?" she pouted. He had been gone all week and she missed him. He was really spoiling her with his time and affection and she hated to go without it.

"You can always come home with me." He offered.

"Well let me pack a bag." She headed to the bedroom to pack her overnight bag. She was excited to spend time with Rico. Sincere was pushed to the back of her mind. She had a good man and wasn't about to mess it up for Sincere. After Reign packed her bag they headed out the door.

"So you know I'm really digging you." Rico whispered in Reigns ear as they cuddled on the couch. She had been with him for the past week totally neglecting everything else. She was slowly pushing Sincere to the back of her mind and making room for Rico. He was such a thug but a gentleman at the same time. He made sure she wanted for nothing and spent time with her. She never had to wonder what her position in his life was.

"I know. I digging you too boo." She leaned up and kissed his cheek.

"I'm glad cause you got a nigga off his square fucking with you." They shared a laugh.

Coming Soon!

http://www.amazon.com/Gangsters-Daughter-5-Leo-Sullivan-ebook/dp/B00NW5WIIW/ref=sr_1_2?ie=UTF8&qid=14117840 72&sr=8-2&keywords=gangster%27s+daughter+5

Out on Kindle

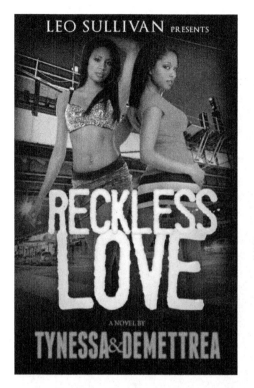

Coming October 17th...

What happens when you finally meet the person you dreamed of your whole life? Welcome to BK and Cali's world.
When sisters Rain and Irish enters their lives unexpectedly it made their decision to leave long time girlfriends Jada and Ebony so much easier.
Rain and Irish might be a dream come true for the young men but with deranged ex's always lurking around these couples doesn't stand a chance of true happiness.
Sometimes letting go isn't as easy as it sounds in this Reckless Love Affair!

Coming October 6th....

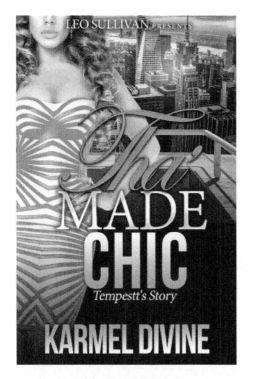

Coming in October....

Coming October 10ᵗʰ...

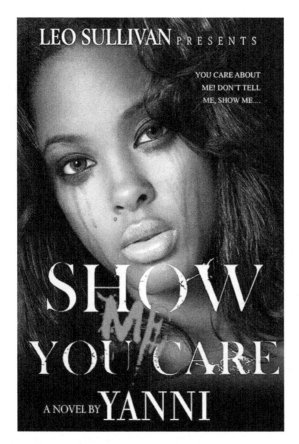

Coming October 13th...

Order Form

Sullivan Productions LLC.

2020 West Pensacola Street, unit 20323, Tallahassee Florida 32316, United States

Name_____

_____

Address_____

_____

City/State_____

_____

Zip_____

Titles	*Price*
A Gangsta's Bitch Pt. 1	*$15.00*
A Gangsta's Bitch Pt. 2	*$15.00*
A Gangsta's Bitch Pt. 3	*$15.00*
A Gangsta's Daughter 1	*$15.00*
A Gangsta's Daughter 2	*$15.00*
A Gangsta's Daughter 3	*$15.00*
A Gangsta's Daughter 4	*$15.00*
Life	*$15.00*
Saving Sierra	*$15.00*

Zero Degrees $15.00

Innocent Revenge $15.00

The Billionairess Thief $15.00

In This Life $15.00

The Cocaine Princess Pt. 1 $15.00

The Cocaine Princess Pt. 2 $15.00

The Cocaine Princess Pt. 3 $15.00

Meesh, Myself, and I $15.00

Dangerously Loving Meesh Pt. 2 $15.00

Dangerously Loving Meesh Pt. 3 $15.00

Meesh Unleashed: The Finale $15.00

Rose City Chic $15.00

Rose City Chic 2 $15.00

Backstabbing Bitches $15.00

Daughters of a King and Queen $15.00

Forbidden Fruit Pt. 1 $15.00

Forbidden Fruit Pt. 2 $15.00

Forbidden Fruit Pt. 3 $15.00

Forbidden Fruit Pt. 4 $15.00

Bout That Life: Diablo's Story $15.00

A Bytch Named Karma $15.00

Allergic to Broke $15.00

Bitchery Pt 1 $15.00

Bitchery Pt 2 $15.00

Bitchery Pt 3 $15.00

Bitchery Pt 4 $15.00

Bitchery Pt 5 $15.00

Grimey Bitch $15.00

Tha' Gangsta's Wife
$15.00

Tha' Made Chic $15.00

The Illest Chick $15.00

Caesar's Charm $15.00

Caesar's Charm 2 $15.00

Down Ass Bitch $15.00

Deranged Loverz $15.00

Fyast Life Pt 1 $15.00

Fyast Life Pt 2 $15.00

The Beast of a Cartel
$15.00

The Bease of a Cartel 2   *$15.00*

Rich Boy Mafia Pt 1   *$15.00*

Rich Boy Mafia Pt 2   *$15.00*

Rich Boy Mafia Pt 3   *$15.00*

Rich Boy Mafia Pt 4   *$15.00*

Addicted To Love   *$15.00*

A Queen's Checkmate Pt 1
$15.00

A Queen's Checkmate Pt 2
$15.00

Love and Betrayal Pt 1
$15.00

Love and Betrayal Pt 2
$15.00

Aint No Love Pt 1   *$15.00*

Aint No Love Pt 2   *$15.00*

Aint No Love Pt 3   *$15.00*

Sex Fiend   *$15.00*

Sabotage Love   *$15.00*

A Boss Chic: Love Story
$15.00

A Boss Chic: 2	*$15.00*
A Boss Chic: 3	*$15.00*
Torn Love	*$15.00*
Torn Love 2	*$15.00*
Smashing Homies	*$15.00*
Heaven Sent	*$15.00*
My Hitta	*$15.00*
Good Girl Torn	*$15.00*
Da Real Housewives of a Trapped King	*$15.00*
Da Real Housewives of a Trapped King 2	*$15.00*
Mob Money	*$15.00*
Unbreakable	*$15.00*
Unbreakable 2	*$15.00*
Unbreakable 3	*$15.00*
Unbreakable 4	*$15.00*
White Face Gangter	*$15.00*

Shipping/Handling (Via U.S. Medial Mail) $4.95

Total $_____

Forms of Accepted Payments:

Postage Stamps, Institutional Checks & Money Orders, all mail in orders take 5-7 Business days to be delivered.

CPSIA information can be obtained
at www.ICGtesting.com
Printed in the USA
LVOW04s0039310116

473031LV00011B/61/P